JEAN ROBINSON

FAR FROM HOME

Complete and Unabridged

LINFORD
Leicester

First published in Great Britain in 2018

First Linford Edition
published 2019

A catalogue record for this book is available
from the British Library.

ISBN 978–1–4448–4230–2

Published by
F. A. Thorpe (Publishing)
Anstey, Leicestershire

Set by Words & Graphics Ltd.
Anstey, Leicestershire
Printed and bound in Great Britain by
T. J. International Ltd., Padstow, Cornwall

This book is printed on acid-free paper

FAR FROM HOME

At 23, Dani has an exciting chance at a new life when her mother Francine invites her to live with her in Paris and join her fashion business. What's more, Dani has fallen in love with Claude, Francine's right-hand man. But it's anything but plain sailing at home in England, where Dani has been living with her father, who is on the edge of a breakdown from stress and doesn't want her to leave. What will Dani choose to do — and is Claude willing to wait while she decides?

1

Slinging her hand luggage over her shoulder, Dani showed her passport to the surly official who scrutinised her face before handing it back.

As she walked through into the waiting area her heart twisted painfully as she recalled her last time with Ryan, the hurt look as she'd told him she wanted to end their relationship, the way he'd walked away when he'd realised she meant it. Now she was on her way to Paris and had to try to push these troubling thoughts from her mind.

Wandering over to a newsagent, she bought a magazine, then decided to pick up a ham roll to eat on the plane. It was only a short flight but she was already hungry after an early breakfast.

Her flight was called and she made her way to the gate. In the queue, tears threatened and a painful emptiness engulfed her. Ryan had said he loved her. Now, even though she knew it had been the right thing to do, it was hard to imagine life without him after seven years together.

Once on board the plane, she found an aisle seat next to a young couple who seemed wrapped up in themselves and wouldn't want to talk to her.

Soon after take-off the stewardess broke into her thoughts, and she forced a smile and ordered a cola. Try as she might to think positively, her mind could not rid itself of the guilty feeling that she had let Ryan down.

★ ★ ★

Her mother Francine was at the airport to meet her and, after lots of hugging, took one of her bags and led her out of the terminal. Dani loved being with her mum. She was so French with her chic dark hair, perfect figure and impeccable dress sense. It was Francine's life, working with beautiful clothes, fashion designers and models.

The car was waiting for them in the pick-up area outside the airport and one look at the young man sitting in the driving seat set Dani's pulse racing. When Francine insisted she sit in the front seat beside him, her mind went into a spin.

'Claude is my right-hand man,' Francine declared as she slid into the back seat.

This gorgeous man sat relaxed with his hands on the wheel, long legs stretching beneath the dashboard. Short hair curled round the back of his neck, his tanned skin dark against his crisp white shirt. Warm, smiling eyes met Dani's and brought a flush to her cheeks. She quickly averted her gaze when she realised she'd been staring.

'Maybe we could drive through the city, then Danielle can see something of Paris,' Francine suggested. 'You would like that, wouldn't you, my dear? It is a very beautiful city and you have not seen it before.'

Dani forced herself to look out of the

window but had difficulty focussing.

As they gradually crept through the slow-moving traffic, Claude pointed ahead. 'There you see the Louvre Museum with its famous pyramid. Inside are the paintings of the Mona Lisa and Venus de Milo. You must visit one day while you are here.'

The building was impressive but Dani was aware only of the soft voice of this Frenchman whose accent was making it difficult for her to concentrate on anything else. As they drove along a beautiful tree lined boulevard alive with cafés and shops, Dani tried desperately to calm herself. This wasn't the way she usually reacted to strangers.

As she watched fashionable ladies strolling along she began to regret not wearing something more stylish herself, instead of the jeans and jacket she had considered suitable for travelling.

Then the towering mass of the Arc de Triomphe put all such thoughts from her mind and brought her to the edge of her seat. Moments later she could hold her delight in no longer.

'There's the Eiffel Tower,' she gasped

Francine laughed. 'We will need more than two weeks for you to see every-thing, but perhaps you will visit all of them, in time.'

Claude was smiling in amusement and Dani fell silent. What must he think of this gauche Englishwoman, getting excited over famous buildings he saw every day?

His smile was good-humoured. 'I think you are impressed with our beautiful city. I feel as you do every time I look at these majestic buildings.'

As their eyes met briefly, something passed between them that took Dani by surprise. She quickly looked away and stared out of the side window, trying to quell the feelings his closeness was stirring in her.

* * *

Francine's apartment was just as Dani had expected, airy and modern. Although she had visited her mum in France regularly since the divorce, Francine had only recently moved to Paris. Claude had dropped them off and now she and Francine were sitting on cane furniture by the large picture window looking out across what seemed to Dani to be the whole of Paris, chatting and eating crusty baguette with cheese and pâté.

By early evening Dani was so tired all she wanted was to creep into the big bed in her lovely bedroom and snuggle under the softest of duvets. As she drifted into sleep, she briefly wondered about her dad, whether he'd cooked himself a decent meal and ironed a shirt for the following morning.

Then her mind turned to thoughts of Claude. Quickly she dismissed them. What was she thinking? She'd only just met the man. But the look he'd given her had lifted her spirits and made her feel alive again, which after the trauma of the last few days was a welcome relief.

The important thing was that she was

here in Paris with her mum and nothing was going to spoil these two weeks.

★ ★ ★

Next morning she woke to spring sunshine pouring in through the open window, and enjoyed the luxury of lying in bed watching gossamer curtains wafting in the breeze. Eventually she swung her legs over the edge of the huge bed, put on the housecoat that hung behind the door and wandered barefoot into the kitchen to the aroma of freshly brewed coffee.

Francine hugged her tightly then held her away. 'You look better already, my dear. You have some colour in your cheeks. You have lost weight.'

'I'll never be as slim as you,' Dani joked, admiring her mum's slender figure.

'And you do not want to be.' Francine gave her a serious look. 'As a model I had to keep thin. Now it is a habit. You have a perfect figure and you must not change.'

'I don't think I could. I love my food too much.'

'So, now for breakfast.'

Dani sat at the wooden table with a pretty checked cloth and waited hungrily for the plate of pastries Francine was assembling.

'Today we go shopping. You will enjoy that? Then we will go down to the River Seine. It's pleasant to walk there, with much to see. Now you eat, or you will not have energy for any of it.'

Dani had so much energy that all she wanted was to get out there and use it all up. But it was no hardship to sink her teeth into warm croissants and cherry jam.

★   ★   ★

The Paris streets were warm with spring sunshine as Dani swung along happily with large bags full of clothes Francine had treated her to.

'Not so fast,' Francine called from a few paces behind. 'These shoes don't allow me to keep up with you.'

Dani, in cropped trousers and pumps, turned and waited. Her mum, elegant as always in the dark suit and cream blouse she had changed into before leaving the apartment, took a few moments to catch up with her.

'I'm sorry, I'm just so happy. I love Paris, I love springtime.' Dani linked arms with Francine and tilted dark shiny curls onto her shoulder. 'And I love being with you. I miss you so much.'

They walked some way along the wide, crowded boulevard then paused to watch a pavement artist at work.

'We will take these bags back to the car then go down to the river. Would you like that?'

Dani gave a radiant smile and again took off, unable to restrain her enthusiasm. With indulgent tolerance, Francine tried to keep pace with her.

★ ★ ★

It was cool by the river as they stood watching boats go by.

'There you see the famous Notre Dame cathedral, our wonderful gothic church,' Francine said, turning and pointing.

Dani stared in awe at the delicate spire that reached into the sky above Paris, and had to stop herself imagining she was with Claude. She shook herself. She was a twenty-three-year-old woman with a successful career and a home with her dad in a small Essex town. Since arriving in Paris, responsibility had slid from her shoulders, and she felt more like a teenage girl again.

'There are so many bridges,' Dani mused as they wandered further along the tree-lined boulevard beside the river and then stopped to watch a tourist boat sliding beneath one. 'The boats are so long. They must seat hundreds.'

'Yes, the bridges are a feature of the city, one of its major attractions. We'll drive over one later.'

Francine guided her down a side

street and into a small square. Once seated beneath a colourful umbrella overlooking a fountain they ordered coffee. Dani couldn't make up her mind which cake she wanted from the selection on offer.

'The almond tarts are very good,' the young waiter advised, giving Dani an indulgent smile.

'The éclairs are even better,' Francine added.

So she had both, enjoying the warmth of the sun as they watched people strolling by.

'It's good to see you happy,' Francine said. 'I feel there is too much troubling you at home.'

Dani felt her chest tighten. She hadn't thought about any of that since meeting Francine at the airport. Suddenly it was all there again and she was struggling to push it from her mind as she sipped the rich, strong coffee.

'Dad can't stand French coffee,' Dani said, determined to lighten the mood again.

'He is a Philistine,' Francine retorted. When Dani went quiet she held off further criticism.

By the time they got back to the apartment they were both tired.

Francine prepared an omelette and salad and they relaxed in the big comfy armchairs.

'Now tell me what is on your mind, Dani.'

Dani gave a knowing smile. Her mum always knew when she had a problem.

'There's something I want to discuss with you,' she said.

'So what is this something?' Dani hesitated. 'Is it your father?'

Dani was quick to respond. 'Not really. He's under a lot of stress at school. He does look tired and drawn at times, but he seems to be coping alright at the moment.'

'Dani, your father has always been like that. I do not think he is suited to teaching.'

'Mum, you can't say that. He's

dedicated to it. The children are no problem for him. It's the new head of department. She's young and he doesn't agree with the changes she's making.'

'And he will not co-operate, is that so? I know how stubborn he can be.' Francine gave an impatient shake of the head.

Dani groaned inwardly. She didn't want the conversation to develop into a character assassination of her dad. But Francine had already dismissed it.

'Your split with Ryan; is that upsetting you?'

Dani sighed. 'It's been difficult. We'd been together since our last year at school, but we'd grown apart. Then he told me he wanted us to get a place together.'

'And that is not what you wanted. But you still care about him, I think.'

Dani sighed. 'He was very upset, but it wouldn't have worked. I just hope he stays the right side of the law now he hasn't got me keeping him in line.' She paused. 'Actually, it's my job I wanted to talk to you about.'

'I thought you were doing well in this bank you work for.'

'I am, but that's part of the problem,' Dani gripped the arms of the chair as she moved forward. 'The higher up I get, the more pressured it becomes. I'm thinking of making a career change, actually.'

'But this is a career you worked so hard for.'

'I know, Mum, and I've tried to make a go of it. But it's not what I thought it would be. I don't enjoy the work any more and recently I've felt I can't carry on.'

'What is it you wish to do?'

'I'm thinking of applying for a job in one of the big department stores in Chelmsford. Alex works in one and she really enjoys what she does. It's what made me realise I'm in the wrong job.'

Francine nodded. 'I hear there are good opportunities in management in some of these big retail stores.'

'That's what I'm aiming for,' Dani said, brightening. 'I'd like to work with people instead of being stuck in an office in front of a computer all day long.' Dani could feel her spirits rising just talking about it.

'I think you are interested in fashion, also. Is that not so?' Francine said.

Dani laughed. 'I wonder who I take after.'

Francine smiled indulgently. 'Not your father.'

Then the smile faded as she leaned forward and took Dani's hand.

'You have a lot on your mind, but you should not act impulsively, my dear. Take your time, consider carefully before you make this change.'

Dani relaxed again. 'Mum, I'm twenty-three. Ryan and I have split up. I still live at home with Dad. I'm in a career I know isn't right for me. My life is going nowhere. I won't do anything irresponsible — you know me better than that — but I have decided to do something about it.'

Francine nodded. 'Then that is good. Trust your own judgement and make your own decisions. Nobody can make them for you.'

Dani felt better after talking it through with Francine — more settled, not so fearful of taking this step, of giving up a safe and steady career to start all over again in something totally different. Francine was so easy to talk to. Unlike her dad.

'Why did you two ever marry?' Dani asked her. It had always puzzled her. Her parents were such different people.

Francine sighed. 'We were very young. I was modelling in London. Your father was at college training to become a teacher. We met at a concert while having a drink before the performance. Your father immediately impressed me with his soft voice and quiet manners. He was so English.'

Dani raised an eyebrow. 'He doesn't have a soft voice now. You should have heard him last week!'

'I think many years in the classroom has changed him.'

'Working in that school would change

anyone,' Dani said with feeling. 'I hated my time there.'

'It is a rough school, I know, but that was his choice, to help these children.'

'Yes, I've heard his theories. Raise the standard of the school. But I was the one who had to put up with all the bad language.'

Francine nodded.

'So what happened after the concert when you and Dad met?' Dani asked.

'We met frequently afterward and were soon married. I found it difficult to adjust, particularly after you were born and my modelling career came to an end. Brandwell is a drab little town.'

'It's certainly not like Paris.' Dani laughed. 'Were you very unhappy?'

Francine sighed. 'Your father was a dedicated teacher and would always put his work first. I spent many lonely evenings while he was ensconced behind a pile of exercise books.'

Dani grunted. 'That hasn't changed. And long country walks studying the wildlife. At least he doesn't insist on me going with him now.'

'I tried hard to make our marriage work, but the arguments became more frequent until I decided that for all our sakes it would be better if I moved out.'

'That was a brave thing to do,'

'It was a heartbreaking decision. I would have liked to take you with me but that would not have been the best thing for you. I knew your father would care for you and it was the right place for you to be.'

'But what did you do when you left? I never really knew. One day you were there, and then the next day Dad was explaining to me that you'd gone to stay with Lou and Nico for a while. When you didn't come back I realised it had to be more than that.'

'At first that was what I did. Fortunately your grandparents had their own fashion house and, as the business was expanding, they were happy to hand over much of it to me. So I stayed and worked hard to build it up. I shall be opening my fourth boutique here in Paris next month.' Francine's expression changed to one of concern. 'You think, perhaps, I was very selfish, thinking only of myself?'

Dani shook her head. 'I never thought that. I just missed you a lot.' Seeing the pain that caused Francine, she wished she hadn't said it.

'Partly, I felt I was preparing the way for you. I knew the life you had in Brandwell would not satisfy you and now I think I was right.'

Francine got up and went to the kitchen to refill their coffee cups.

Dani frowned. What did her mum mean? Her life was in Brandwell. She couldn't imagine living anywhere else. But a little spark of optimism began to rise in her. Was it possible?

'And I have the lovely Claude to help me,' Francine called through.

'What does he actually do?' Dani tried to keep her voice matter-of-fact and failed miserably. She'd been dying to bring the subject up but felt self-conscious about it, afraid she'd expose her feelings too openly and Francine would catch on.

'He's very talented and will turn his hand to any aspect of the business. Your grandfather knew his family and took him on as soon as he left college. Then when I moved here to Paris he sent him to me to help me set up this branch of the business. He works so hard. I could not have accomplished what I have done without him.'

'How long will he stay?' Dani said it before she could stop herself. Her grandparents, Lou and Nico, lived far from Paris and she didn't want Claude disappearing as soon as she'd met him. Then she pulled herself up short. She was only here for two weeks.

'I think for some time yet,' Francine said, giving Dani a searching look as she came back into the room carrying two cups of coffee. 'He is popular with the designers,' she continued as she handed a cup to Dani. 'And the models all love him and will do anything to please him. They are a temperamental lot so it is good to have him to keep them in line.'

Dani knew there was no way she could slot into a world like this. She had business qualifications but they certainly had nothing to do with fashion. Her life was in Brandwell. She'd start looking for an opening in one of the big department stores in Chelmsford, then as soon as she could afford it, she'd get a flat of her own. She wanted her life to change . . . but she had to be realistic.

When they'd finished their coffee, Francine got up and took Dani's hand to help her from the chair. 'Now we must rest. I have a busy day planned for you tomorrow.'

Dani hugged her mum then made her way to her lovely room with the comfy bed. Lying in the dark, thoughts drifted in and out of her mind. What had Francine really meant when she'd said she was preparing the way for her? Did she plan that one day Dani would work in the fashion business with the rest of the family? The thought of seeing Claude every day made her heart beat faster — but that wasn't going to happen. Her home was in Brandwell, with her dad. There could be no place for her in a top fashion house in Paris.

2

The next day was sheer magic. Francine whisked Dani from office to factory, through store rooms packed with beautiful clothes. She watched designers sketch outrageously exciting shapes for next season's gowns, overheard the chatter on phones and between the staff and saw how right her mother was among it all.

They were preparing for a show to launch a new range of clothes and tension was mounting. Final adjustments had to be made to the garments. Pierre, the young designer, was prancing around, eyes darting critically from collar to hem then erupting in either horror or delight.

By noon Dani was so absorbed in this fascinating world that all thoughts of home were forgotten.

'This afternoon I must work in my

office so I'll ask Claude to take you to visit our boutiques,' Francine explained as she and Dani lunched in a small patisserie.

Dani couldn't quite believe what she was hearing. Spending a whole afternoon with Claude would be nerve-racking, yet she was unable to quell the bubble of excitement rising inside her.

★　★　★

Looking into Claude Duval's dark eyes as he led her out of Francine's office an hour later did nothing to calm her nerves. But she was soon absorbed in the boutiques he took her to see. They were spread around the various fashion districts of Paris where very rich women came for designer clothes, each boutique spacious and furnished to create an ambience of luxury. The assistants were friendly and keen to impress Dani, and she could not have wished for a more attentive escort than Claude. Although only in his late twenties, he took responsibility easily with a maturity her friends back home in England lacked.

'We were lucky to get him,' the manager of one boutique whispered to Dani. 'He is so talented and well respected. I think we could not have managed without his hard work when we began to open up these boutiques in Paris.'

When Claude handed Dani back to Francine in her office late that afternoon she was all fired up and, although she knew it was an impossible dream, wishing with all her heart that she could be part of this exciting world.

Francine was studying some papers she had received in the post and Dani went to sit at the desk beside her. The office was small with two desks, a filing cabinet and shelves full of catalogues and glossy fashion magazines, folders full of photos and samples of materials.

Claude went to the computer at the other desk and sat in front of it, frowning.

The phone rang and, after a short conversation, Francine put it down and got up.

'I must find some photos for this magazine. The editor wants them urgently to meet his deadline.' She looked at Dani and hesitated. 'Maybe you can help Claude? He is not good with this new program we have installed.'

Dani froze. Sitting beside Claude would disrupt her concentration and even though she was confident with computers, she felt sure she would not be able to sort whatever it was that was causing him a problem. Francine had put her on the spot and she had no option but to do as she had asked. Claude smiled up at her as she perched on the stool beside him. As soon as she saw what he was trying to do her heart gave a leap of joy.

'Oh, that's no problem.' It was something she could easily fix.

He swivelled his chair to one side so she could sit in front of the screen.

'Then maybe you can explain this program for me. Whatever I do it seems determined not to let me proceed.'

She soon had the pages he needed up on the screen and talked him through the procedure.

Claude gave an appreciative smile and she couldn't keep a satisfied smirk from her face.

'And are you as proficient in accounting? It is difficult for me, this subject,' he said.

'I work for a bank,' she replied.

'Such a pretty woman, and so clever, too.'

She felt her colour rise at his cheeky smile.

'Now I embarrass you. You must forgive me. I am surrounded by beautiful women all day, but none so clever as you.'

They both looked towards the door when a tall, willowy redhead with huge blue eyes came into the room. She took in the situation and gave Dani a look that made her shrivel inside.

Claude stood up and went towards her and they kissed on both cheeks.

'This is Danielle, Francine's daughter. I have been showing her our boutiques,' he told her, then turned to Dani. 'Rêve is one of our models.'

Rêve gave Dani another withering look then glanced at the screen where Claude had been working. 'You are having problems again, I see,' she said, giving Claude a knowing smile.

'I was,' Claude admitted. 'But now I have a new assistant who works in a bank and is expert at these things. I do not need to worry any more. Danielle will help me.' He looked towards Dani. 'Am I right?'

Dani smiled and nodded but felt uncomfortable with the way Claude was talking about her, as if he were joking at her expense. And this glamorous woman obviously didn't like the attention being taken from her.

Rêve started to talk to Claude in French and he listened for a while then looked annoyed.

'Dani can speak French as well and you and me,' he said.

Dani wasn't quite as fluent as he suspected but she'd got the gist of the conversation. Rêve thought Dani had no place in the business and hoped she wasn't going to be a distraction while they were busy getting the fashion show together.

There followed an angry exchange between Claude and Rêve, none of which Dani understood as they were speaking fast and sometimes both together. Claude flung his arms in the air in frustration. Rêve stopped shouting and began to sulk. Dani backed off and sat rigid in the seat Francine had vacated, wishing her mum would hurry up and come back.

In the end Rêve flounced out of the office and Claude sat down opposite Dani, his expression as black as thunder.

'She is very rude, that girl,' he said to Dani.

'Can't say I warmed to her,' Dani said.

'I will have words with her. She cannot behave like this.'

'I think she has a problem with me helping you,' Dani said, her hands trembling.

'She is jealous, that is all.'

'But why would she be jealous of me?'

'Because I tell her how clever you are. And you are Francine's daughter.' He took her shaking hands in his.

His concern comforted her but she didn't want her mum coming in and seeing them like this together. It would only raise awkward questions.

'Claude, don't mention any of this to Mum.'

'Why not?' he asked sternly.

She drew her hands from his. 'Because I don't want to cause trouble as soon as I arrive. I can cope with Rêve.'

He pulled his chair back but his eyes never left her. 'Danielle, you should not have to cope with Rêve's bad behaviour. But I will not tell your mother. I will deal with it. It will not happen again.'

★   ★   ★

Back in the apartment that evening Francine asked Dani what all the shouting was about while she was out of the office.

'I could hear their raised voices.'

Dani began to unload the dish-washer. She really didn't want to get into this conversation.

'I don't know, Mum. They were speaking in French and I didn't catch much of it.'

Francine sighed as she topped up the coffee machine. 'That girl; she is so temperamental. It takes nothing to upset her. But she's good on the catwalk — not just her figure, but the way she moves, the way she tosses her head, her smile, her pout. She is worth the trouble.'

'She certainly does a lot of pouting,' Dani said, then realised how catty it sounded and wished she'd kept her thoughts to herself.

Francine shook her head as she took cups from the cupboard. 'I don't know how Claude copes with her. I think maybe he's rather taken with her, and she does as he asks most of the time, which is good.'

Dani turned her face to the window as she felt her heart plummet. She could see now exactly what had happened. Rêve knew Claude had been escorting her round Francine's boutiques all afternoon and felt they were getting too friendly and, as Francine's daughter, she could take advantage of her position. Claude had felt obliged to defend Dani. He and Rêve were probably laughing about it now as they sipped wine together in a bistro after work.

She was brought out of her reverie by Francine standing in front of her. 'Now, my dear, what do you think? Would you like to be part of all this?'

Dani stared at her. 'What?'

'Im asking if you would like to come here and work with me. You said you wanted a change of career. So why not come to Paris and see if this life is more to your liking?'

Dani couldn't take in what Francine was offering. It seemed as if what she had been dreaming about was becoming a possibility.

'You mean you want me to come here and live with you and work with you, instead of looking for another job at home?'

'That is what I am asking. Do you want that?'

All thoughts of Claude and Rêve disappeared. Dani wanted more than anything to be part of this prestigious fashion house Francine was building.

'Yes, I'd love to, but . . . '

'Then it is settled. You must go home and speak with your father, give your notice to the bank and arrange to come back here.'

'But, Mum, I don't know anything at all about fashion or modelling.'

Francine dismissed this with a toss of her head. 'You will learn.'

Dani wasn't so sure after the way Rêve had treated her, however. Could she really become part of this scene?

'My dear, I understand how you feel. But you are already an asset to this business with the knowledge you have. I saw how you helped Claude with his project planning on the computer this afternoon. And you understand accounting. We need your expertise here.'

Dani brightened. She was beginning to see how the skills she had acquired could help.

'And you'll be able to deal with our overseas customers who speak only English,' Francine added excitedly.

'Yes, global supply chains, international marketing,' Dani mused, now full of enthusiasm.

Francine beamed at her. 'You see, my dear, you are just what we need now we're expanding our business abroad.'

Dani's confidence was rising. All her knowledge could be put to good use in the family business. Her mum needed her. Claude needed her. Everything she had studied was relevant to the life she wanted to live here in Paris.

'So, will you join our team?' Francine asked.

Francine made it sound so easy, but to Dani it was an enormous step to take. She had lived in Brandwell all her life, running the home she lived in with her dad. All her friends were there. What her mum was offering was a career in a business she had no knowledge of, in a country she had only visited for holidays!

'Mum, I need time to think about it. I can't just drop everything and come.'

Francine's face softened. 'Of course you can't. You must go home and think it through, then make your decision. I won't pressure you.'

Dani relaxed. This would give her time to get used to the idea . . . although she knew deep down she was going to make it happen, that this was the life she wanted.

She hugged Francine excitedly. 'But I want to stay for the rest of this holiday.'

'And you will. I still have much to show you.'

★ ★ ★

During the following days Francine was busier than ever and Dani was anxious to help wherever she could, trying to get a feel of how it all worked and decide if she really could fit in and make a contribution to the business. As the week progressed she began to see more and more how the skills and knowledge she had would be useful and her enthusiasm grew.

'Tomorrow you are not working,' Francine said one evening as they sat after their meal. 'I have asked Claude to take you to see some of the sights you want to see. I don't have the time, and he's young and will be able to keep up with you.'

The thought of spending the day with Claude both thrilled and alarmed her. She still didn't know what his relationship with Rêve was and she couldn't bear to think of him being ordered to look after her as part of his job.

Yet he had seemed genuinely concerned about what had happened, so she made up her mind not to let the episode with Rêve upset her. She would take advantage of the day out and enjoy Claude's company. So long as she didn't let her feelings run away with her, no harm could come of it. It would be an opportunity to see more of Paris and get a feel of the city she was now hoping to live and work in.

★ ★ ★

'This is what we call our rest room,' Francine explained the next day as she ushered Dani into a large room next to the office to wait for Claude.

Dani thought it a lovely room, furnished with old leather sofas, mismatched and peeling. Colourful rugs were strewn on the wooden floor and a gas heater hissed from the far wall. Samples of materials, photos of models and sketches of dresses were piled on the low tables, and there were garments draped on hooks round the walls. In one corner a coffee machine gurgled. It was hot and stuffy, with little light filtering through the cracked windows. To Dani it was part of this new world she was beginning to understand and love.

Francine phoned to let Claude know they had arrived. Eventually the sound of raised voices drew closer and Claude came into the room, followed by Rêve and a very distraught Pierre. Claude was obviously trying to ignore the argument between the other two. Pierre and Rêve were shouting at each other and neither was listening to the other.

'I will not wear this sack!' Rêve shrieked at Pierre. Then she turned to Claude. 'You must tell him. You do not expect me to take to the catwalk in such a monstrosity?'

They seemed unaware of Francine and Dani standing beside the coffee machine. Francine shook her head in despair as she and Dani watched the scene unfold before her.

Claude put up a pacifying hand and tried to halt their progress into the room. 'No, of course not. Pierre, you must fix this dress to fit properly.'

'It does fit correctly. It is the style,' he wailed.

The short, flared dress Rêve was now wearing was a startling pink and showed off her long shapely legs to perfection. She pointed at the garment Pierre was shaking in the air.

'That is not a style. It is a sack!' she screamed, her face so flushed it almost matched her dress.

Pierre was red in the face too and not willing to give in. 'She does not know what she talks about. I know fashion. She is just to show it off.'

Rêve looked up at Claude. 'I am not wearing it,' she said defiantly. 'It is ugly and not my colour. He must use one of the others to show off this dress. I will not make myself look a fool.' Then she noticed Francine and burst into tears.

Claude went to her and she leaned into him, resting her head on his chest. His arms slipped round her as he tried to calm her.

'No one will make you wear what you do not feel comfortable in. We will find something else.'

Pierre watched, muttered something under his breath, threw the offending dress into the corner of the room and stomped out. Francine indicated to Dani that they should leave and led her down the passage and into the office.

'Claude will sort it,' she told Dani. 'Rêve will do as he says once she's calmed down. Pierre and Rêve often have these tempestuous times, then next day all is sunny again.' She smiled at Dani. 'It is artistic temperament, I believe.'

Dani thought it was just plain stupid and that Rêve was behaving like a spoilt child! It confirmed her fears and any hopes she had of spending an enjoyable day with Claude evaporated. What she had suspected was true — he was going to be lumbered with her for the afternoon when he'd so obviously rather spend it with Rêve.

3

Dani sat beside Claude as he drove through the outskirts of Paris and her unease slowly evaporated, leaving in its place a warm, happy feeling. She couldn't help taking a sideways glance at him. He had an air of confidence and was easily the most handsome man she had ever set eyes on. She liked the relaxed way his hands rested on the wheel as he wove in and out of the Paris traffic, then swung into a car park and slid into the nearest space without fuss.

She knew she had to keep her head but was determined not to let the incident with Rêve spoil her day. There was no reason why she and Claude could not be friends and enjoy this outing.

'From now on we take the Metro,' Claude said as he opened the door to let her out. 'Parking in this city is not easy.'

'Fine, I'm used to walking.'

'You like to walk? We can see more by walking.'

She laughed. 'I've been doing it all my life. My dad thinks there's no other way of getting around. He used to drag me out in all weathers for what he called a healthy bit of exercise. I reckon I've walked hundreds of miles of the Essex countryside in my life.'

He put a hand to her back to guide her across a busy road and it felt warm and good. 'A little more would not be disagreeable, then?'

'Paris would be lot more fun than the woods round Brandwell.'

'And a few steps? You do not mind climbing a little?' His dark eyes were smiling.

'Fine by me,' she said, glad she'd worn her jeans and sandals and put her curls in a ponytail. The sun was warm so she'd taken her her jacket off and tied it round her waist. When their bare arms touched, she gave an involuntary shiver and quickly moved aside a little.

But as they continued to walk she could still feel that tingle right down to her fingertips.

Claude was dressed in a casual shirt and trousers but Dani couldn't imagine him ever stepping into a pair of trainers. The slight shadow on his face showed he would have a strong, dark beard if he chose to grow one.

'The Metro's a lot cleaner and brighter than the Underground in London,' Dani said as they stood waiting for the train.

'It is not so old, I think. Built only in 1900.'

'That sounds pretty old to me,' she laughed.

The few steps Claude had mentioned turned out to be rather a lot and Dani was out of breath when they got to the top of Montmartre — but also enthralled with everything she saw. The whole place was alive and noisy with artists selling paintings, cafés and bars and lots of people. They stopped to look at a stall where antique jewellery was displayed on a blue velvet cloth.

'I would like you to choose something, Dani — a present from me.'

She pulled back. 'Oh, no, I'm just admiring it.'

'Please, Dani, it would give me great pleasure.'

'No, Claude, really I was just looking, although it's very beautiful.'

'Then I will choose,' he said, picking up a bracelet of coloured stones set in ovals of silver. Once he'd paid for it, he took Dani's hand and fastened the bracelet round her wrist. Looking from the bracelet into those deep dark eyes, Dani felt a great surge of pleasure.

As they meandered on she kept stopping to look at other stalls. One displaying clothes in beautiful colours and patterns took her eye. Then, looking up, she stopped and gasped.

'There's the Moulin Rouge!'

He stood beside her and put an arm round her shoulders as she stared in delight.

'I've seen pictures of it with its big red windmill and now I'm standing right in front of it.'

He laughed. 'Our famous theatre. I think you are enjoying this outing.'

Further up the steps and they were standing in front of the most beautiful building Dani had ever seen, white and mellow in the afternoon light and looking very much like pictures she had seen of the Taj Mahal.

'It is the Basilique de Sacre Coeur,' Claude declared solemnly. 'From the top of the dome you can view all of Paris.'

They went inside and Claude crossed himself, closing his eyes in silent prayer. She stood beside him, feeling the gravity of the place, then he led her further into its majestic interior.

'Now, look up and you will see a mosaic ceiling which is the largest in the world.'

She had to force herself to believe this was real. Here she was in this magnificent building with Claude. His nearness produced feelings she hadn't experienced before and she wondered if this was what love felt like. She also felt very vulnerable. Claude stood in front of her, his look at first questioning, then their eyes locked and it was an age before the spell was broken and they reluctantly tried to refocus on where they were.

'Dani, what is the matter?'

She shrugged uncomfortably.

'Oh, it's nothing. I don't know . . . '

'I think I do. I think you wonder about me and Rêve. Is that not so?'

She looked directly at him and nodded.

'I don't want to get involved in any of this.'

'Any of what?'

She shook her head. 'Any of this bad feeling.'

'There is no bad feeling. I have to look after the people who work for us. It's what your mother pays me to do.'

Looking him straight in the eye she took a deep breath. 'And is she paying you to look after me?'

His expression told her she'd really

upset and annoyed him now and she looked away, trying to hide her emotions.

He turned her to face him.

'I would not play games with you. Rêve is a tiresome employee I must deal with. Part of my job is to get the best out of the people working with us. She's a good model and I want her in this next show. That's all.'

Dani looked up at him, their eyes locking.

'And what about me?'

'I want to be with you, Dani.'

She gave a tentative smile.

'Do you believe me?' he asked, his expression earnest.

She nodded and her smile became warm.

'But surely Pierre is more important than Rêve? After all, he actually makes the clothes,' she said, trying to get things on an even keel again, conscious that people around were beginning to take notice of them.

Claude relaxed and took her hand as

they continued to walk round the building.

'Of course, but Pierre will not flounce off and leave if he doesn't get his own way. He is loyal to your mother.'

'I can see why Mum values you so much.'

Outside again, the air was warm.

'Now we take a walk along the river, I think.'

Her happiness was restored. 'At this rate we'll see the whole of Paris in one day.'

They ambled back down the steps and were soon on a path beside the River Seine.

'I love this walk. We keep close to the river and walk under the bridges. I think however many times I do it I would never tire of it,' he told her.

'So many bridges, so many boats,' she mused.

'Yes, many tourist boats. I will take you sometime. Maybe one evening. It is so romantic in the moonlight.'

Dani felt a blush warm her face as she looked into deep, dark eyes that held hers. She pulled away from his gaze knowing she mustn't let her emotions run away with her. Maybe he did enjoy her company for an afternoon — but someone like Rêve was definitely more in his league.

He stopped, his voice now one of concern.

'You are tired. I have dragged you everywhere and never stopped.'

'I wouldn't mind a sit down, for just a minute,' she admitted.

He took her hand and they were off again. 'So, we'll go to the rooftop of Samaritaine, where you may have some of your wonderful English tea.'

After another Metro journey and they were sitting above the whole of Paris and she couldn't believe the view.

'You certainly know your way around.'

'Not many tourists can find this place, so it's special. It's the best view of the Eiffel Tower you will ever see, especially in this spring sunshine.'

When they'd finished their tea they walked back across one of the many bridges, dodging roller skaters and cyclists. Everywhere was busy and noisy and it made Dani feel alive and light-hearted.

As dusk settled over the river they stopped to watch the buildings and bridges glowing warmly in the setting sun.

'Now I will take you home,' he said, and she felt a deep twinge of disappointment.

* * *

During the following days Dani went everywhere with Francine, finding out as much as she could about the work and helping where possible. She became more and more certain this was the life she wanted. The thought of continuing with the bank was now out of the question. She would embark on this new life, one she could put all her efforts into knowing it was for her family.

Between times they relaxed in the apartment or, when Francine could spare the time, went into the city so Dani could absorb the beauty of the buildings and stare in awe at the shop windows.

She had been trying to sort out photos for Francine one afternoon and needed to go into the rest room for folders.

When she opened the door, what she saw made her gasp and quickly back out. Claude was sitting opposite Rêve holding both her hands and staring into her eyes, totally unaware of Dani. Rêve was dabbing her face with a tissue and Claude's face was drawn in concentration. He was talking to her in his soft French accent, soothing and gentle.

Dani stood outside shaking, her feet rooted to the spot. She couldn't bring herself to interrupt such an apparently intimate moment and her feeling of betrayal was impossible to ignore. Yet if she went back without the folders Francine would want to know why.

She straightened up and took a deep breath. Pushing open the door noisily with her foot, she walked in.

'Sorry to disturb you,' she said in a loud voice. 'Just carry on and pretend I'm not here.' Speaking in this forced cheerful voice was the only way she could cope with the situation. She grabbed what she needed and got out as quickly as she could without looking at either of them.

Once in the passageway again she stopped, her heart thumping wildly. She had to gain control before she went back into the office with the folders.

Suddenly, Claude was standing in front of her. With every bit of strength she could muster she pushed past him and strode towards the office, put the folders on the table for Francine and somehow managed to speak in a normal voice.

For the rest of the afternoon Dani worked furiously at the filing cabinet Francine had said needed to be sorted out. The contents had to be scanned into the computer for storage. All the time Dani tried to concentrate fully on what she was doing but was continually chiding herself for her stupidity in reading more into Claude's approaches than was obviously meant. She repeatedly told herself it was just his manner.

He probably flirted with all the women he came in contact with. Francine had told her as much. She should have taken it in her stride and not let her emotions get out of hand.

When Francine suggested she take a break she refused, saying she was interested in what she was finding out about the business and that she'd prefer to continue until the job was done.

'But Dani, you have been at it for two hours non-stop now.'

'Mum, I go home tomorrow. I want to finish the job. I'm nearly done now.'

Francine smiled indulgently. 'You are a keen worker. It will be good to have you here with us.'

Dani managed a smile and continued to work her way through the material in the folders.

She wasn't sure now that moving to

Paris was what she wanted after all. To work with Claude every day, knowing he and Rêve were close and she would always be an outsider, wasn't a comfortable feeling. Probably her best bet was to go home and find other work there, as she had planned, treat her stay here as an experience and forget all about Paris.

However, then she would be giving in to her own stupidity. No, Paris was where she wanted to be. It was a great opportunity for her to have a satisfying career without wasting any of her business qualifications. She knew she should not let any man stop her from her goal.

It was when they were about to go home after looking through sketches Pierre had produced that the phone rang.

After a brief conversation, Francine smiled and handed it to Dani.

Claude's voice set her insides churning.

'I would like to take you out tonight.

It is my friend's birthday and we will celebrate. You will enjoy the evening, I think.'

How could he use this tone with her when he knew how much he'd upset her? Then again, he didn't know he'd upset her. It was all in her mind. He had told her he enjoyed being with her, not that he was madly in love with her! The fact that she had fallen for his charm was hardly his fault. And how could she turn him down without baring her heart to Francine, something she was not ready to do? She had to deal with this in a mature way and not let her emotions rule her head and spoil her future here in Paris.

Francine was smiling and Dani gripped the phone and bit hard on her lips to stop them trembling. She had to get a grip.

Claude was inviting her out for an evening. He was being friendly. She didn't want to go with him to this party, especially if Rêve was there as well, but it was her last evening before going home and she didn't want to leave with bad feeling between them. She had to put their relationship on the right footing so they could work together when she came back. Seeing him this evening would be her best chance.

He'd noticed the pause.

'Dani, we need to talk,' he said quietly.

'Yes,' she managed.

'I will pick you up at eight.'

Slowly she returned the phone to Francine.

'It will be good for you to have some young company,' Francine said.

Dani managed a smile but her heart was heavy.

Back in the apartment, Rêve's behaviour crept into the conversation as Dani was changing into the new jeans and top Francine had bought for her. She wasn't in the mood for dressing up. She just wanted to get the evening over with.

'I hear Claude had another fracas with Rêve this afternoon. I wonder how long we can keep humouring her. She is so tiresome,' Francine said as she viewed

Dani with approval.

'She's certainly got Claude where she wants him,' Dani said with feeling.

'Oh, all the ladies love Claude and he charms them with his manners and his good looks.'

Well, I'm not going to be one of them, Dani thought.

'However, we have a business to run and cannot forever be worrying whether our models will walk out before a show and leave us short,' Francine continued.

Dani wasn't listening. She could hardly bear the hurt she was feeling. Did Claude see her as just another of his many admirers? He obviously thrived on it. However hard she tried to subdue her feelings those dark eyes haunted her.

Francine brushed a dark curl from her forehead. 'Be careful, my dear, that you do not fall for his charm. I think you enjoy being with him but I do not want you to get hurt.'

Dani smiled with a confidence she didn't feel, desperately trying to hide her emotions.

'Mum, I know the score, so don't worry.'

★   ★   ★

Claude picked her up in his car and they drove into the city. Both seemed intent on keeping the conversation light and impersonal. Nothing was said about the incident with Rêve.

He parked the car under some trees and opened the door for her to get out. They didn't look at each other. They were careful not to touch. He placed his arm lightly on her back to lead her towards a tree-lined path that slowly meandered high above the city. He then quickly dropped his arm to his side. As they walked along he kept a distance between them, sensing that was the way she wanted it.

The atmosphere was tense.

When Dani tried to lighten it with comments about the beauty of the evening, determined to keep things as casual as possible between them, Claude said little.

After agonising moments of silence, he stopped and turned her to look through the trees at the setting sun. She felt an involuntary shiver at the touch of his hand on her shoulder and swallowed hard as she saw in the distance the dark silhouette of the Eiffel Tower set against the deepening blue of a twilight sky.

'This is a peaceful place where we can talk,' he said at last.

She was too choked to speak.

He turned her to face him and her heart was almost breaking when she saw the solemn expression on his face. Why had he brought her to this romantic place to tell her that she meant nothing to him, that it was all in her mind?

He took her hands and she didn't resist. His voice was soft.

'Danielle, I want to explain . . . '

She tried hard to control her feelings, to follow her plan to keep everything business-like and friendly, but it was hopeless with those deep, dark eyes devouring her.

'Go ahead,' she murmured, tensing

herself for the inevitable.

He swallowed and seemed to be composing himself, as if what he had to say was difficult. She wished he'd just get it over with. Then he could take her home and she could go to her room and have a good cry.

When he spoke his voice was soft and gentle and barely audible.

'What you saw this afternoon was not what it appeared to be. I'm afraid Rêve had the wrong impression about my feelings for her and I had to put her right. She was upset. That's when you came into the room.'

Dani was trying to hang on to her resolve. She would not let him play her as he did all these beautiful adoring women.

'You looked very cosy to me,' she managed, trying to keep the tremble from her voice.

'I was trying to let her down gently, Danielle.' His expression became more intense.

'Well, you don't need to let me down

gently. I've already worked it out.'

'Actually, I told Rêve how I felt about you.'

'I'm sure that cheered her up no end.' She could hardly get the words out as her voice kept choking up.

His grip on her hands tightened and she could not mistake the look in his eyes.

'Danielle, you are not listening to me. You are determined to think badly of me. I have known you only two weeks, but we have spent much time together and . . . well, I think I'm falling in love with you. That is what I told Rêve.'

Tears began to trickle down her cheeks and he pulled her to him and held her tightly. In those strong arms she felt loved.

'Do you think you could love me, too?' he murmured.

'I don't know, Claude . . . ' she managed.

He kissed her tenderly, then more passionately as they remained locked together for long moments.

When he took her hand and led her back down the path through the trees the sun had slipped towards the horizon, setting the Eiffel Tower in dark relief against a crimson sky.

Her happiness was overflowing, and she knew in that moment that she was in love.

4

An hour later they emerged from the station into a run-down area of the city and Dani gripped Claude's hand more firmly. In the dark she could just about see the peeling paint and rusted drain-pipes on the buildings, their shutters hanging at strange angles.

As they walked past tenement blocks in serious need of renovation, Dani wondered where they were going and why Claude had brought her to such a place.

He sensed her unease and slowed down until they were a little behind Maurice and other friends they'd met in a bar earlier.

'This is Belleville where artists live, very cheap. It's all they can afford until they are established. They're good people, Dani — not wealthy but talented. I have known Maurice since I was a child. He lived near my village and we went to school together. Then he came to Paris to study art and one day he will be a famous painter, I think.' His smile relaxed her.

After walking for about ten minutes they met Maurice, a stocky little man with a jolly disposition, who led them around a corner and pulled open a heavy wooden door. Inside, a long corridor led to stairs with a small studio apartment at the top, its door held ajar. Inside, candles created a warm atmosphere. Young people were sitting on the floor listening to a girl with a long skirt tucked round her legs reading poetry.

A couple jumped up to greet them and others in the room looked round and waved. Maurice was surprised and delighted at the gathering and was soon being made a great fuss of.

'These two live above in another room,' Claude explained. 'They knew it was Maurice's birthday and he would bring us here tonight, so they made this surprise for him.'

There was lots of kissing and introductions as they were drawn into the circle. Easels and paintings stood among a selection of old sofas, and a table in one corner had food laid out.

Other young people dropped in during the evening. One brought a guitar and they began to sing. Claude was at ease and enjoying the company yet constantly checking Dani was happy.

'See who has just arrived,' Claude said, turning to Dani. 'I was hoping she would drop in as it's one of the reasons I wanted to bring you here. She is from England too. She's here studying art and lives only a few doors away.'

Nancy was small with short dark hair and a lively face. She seemed to know everyone and, when she saw Claude, she immediately came over and hugged him.

'This is Dani,' Claude said, disentangling himself. 'She is from England and has come here to visit.' Turning to Dani he said. 'This is Nancy, my very good friend.' Nancy's smile was warm and, when she began to talk in fluent, unaccented English, Dani was surprised at how good it felt.

The two girls spent a lot of time together during the evening. Dani sensed that Nancy was someone she could confide in and soon found herself explaining about her mum and dad and the situation she was in.

'Do you think you will come and live over here, then?' Nancy asked.

'I hope so. I'm working for a bank at the moment but I'm thinking of moving on, looking for something else. Mum wants me to work in the family business here.'

'It certainly sounds like much more fun than a fusty old bank!'

They both laughed. It was so like the girlie chats Dani had with Alex and, with a sudden pang of homesickness, she realised how much she would miss her friends if she did come to live in Paris.

When eventually Nancy moved away to talk to some of the others, Claude was immediately at Dani's side. 'We can leave any time if you wish.'

'No, I don't want to go yet. They're nice people and it's good to meet some of your friends. I really like Nancy.'

He gave her an appreciative smile. 'Good, I thought you would. So long as you are happy.'

There was more music and laughter. A small group were huddled in one corner comparing paintings and various techniques and media they used. Dani could tell there was a lot of talent there. The artistic buzz made her feel alive and her doubts quickly vanished as she was again filled with enthusiasm for her future.

'I hear you're in the fashion business,' Maurice said, sitting beside her with a beer in his hand.

She laughed. 'Hardly! But my mum is, and I may join her eventually.'

'This is a good place to be. Paris is one of the most exciting cities in the world for art. You'll be in good company here.'

'Yes, I feel it already,' Dani said.

'This whole city becomes your classroom. My course takes me to museums and art galleries. I've even painted in the Louvre.'

Dani began to feel she could become part of this scene so easily.

Eventually things quietened down as people began to leave, and once more Claude was at her side.

'Do you want to go now? I don't know about you, but I'm starving and there's not much food in this place. We will find somewhere to eat. Would you like that?'

'Yes, I'm hungry, too. Let's go,' she agreed.

She found Nancy in the tiny kitchen off the studio and they exchanged phone numbers and email addresses with a promise to keep in touch. Dani wasn't going to lose contact with her first real friend in France — not when she had more or less decided she was coming back here to live.

'You don't know how lucky you are, Dani, having family here,' Nancy told her. 'I can only stay for a year. It's all I can afford but I'm grateful for that. I'm absorbing a new culture as well as becoming fluent in French.'

'What will you do after your year?' Dani asked.

'Go back to dreary Norfolk, I suppose.' Nancy laughed. Then she became more serious. 'I want to get into photography if I can. This course I'm doing is very comprehensive and I knew straight away when I was photographing the Seine bridges that it was what I wanted. It gave me such a thrill standing there pointing my camera at that wonderful architecture.' Her eyes were dreamy. 'What about you? Do you want to design wonderful gowns?'

Dani laughed. 'No, I don't have the talent for that! But I would like to be part of it all. I'll find a niche where I can be useful, something on the business side. I don't know yet. It's early days.'

'Well, don't lose your dream, Dani.'

Nancy hugged her and looked pensive when Dani left with Claude.

Claude took her to one of his favourite bistros. Tables in cosy corners were covered in red checked cloths with candles giving a warm glow. He took her hand across the small table and, seeing the love in his eyes, she wondered why she had ever doubted him.

'I can't believe this is happening,' she said.

'I feel the same,' he said softly. 'But I knew from the moment I first saw you that we had something special.'

When they got back to Francine's apartment they stood outside in the moonlight and Claude took Dani in his arms and kissed her gently.

'Well, I suppose this is it for a while,' she said as they drew apart.

'I know.' There was sadness in his eyes and in his voice. 'You leave tomorrow.'

'Don't worry, I'll be back.' She knew for certain now that it was what she wanted. 'Then maybe one day I can be your accountant,' she joked.

He gave a wistful smile. 'You will always be more than that to me.'

'It won't be long. I have to sort things with my dad first and hand in my notice in at the bank.'

Claude looked deep into her eyes. 'And I will be waiting for you, my little English rose.'

They hugged tightly, not wanting to part, then he quickly disentangled himself and walked down the steps in front of the apartment.

★ ★ ★

Francine was waiting up for Dani.

'I think you have enjoyed this evening,' she said, a shadow touching her face.

'I've had a wonderful time,' Dani said enthusiastically. 'I met some of Claude's friends at a party and then we went to a lovely little bistro later to eat. I just love Paris.'

Francine's frown deepened as she paused.

'Dani, I hope you are not getting too fond of Claude. I must tell you that he charms all the girls, so you must be careful. Do not make your decision to come and work here in Paris simply so that you can be with him.'

Dani quickly tried to quell the euphoria she was feeling. She hadn't realised it was so obvious.

'No, Mum, I'm coming here to work. It's what I really want to do. Claude has nothing to do with it. He's just a friend.' She wasn't ready to bare her heart to her mum just yet.

Francine came sat beside her. 'That's good. So now you will go home and then as soon as you can, come back here to Paris and begin your new life.'

A sudden fit of panic struck her as Francine spelt out the reality of what was about to happen.

'I hope Dad will be OK with it,' Dani mused. 'It will mean leaving him on his own . . . '

Francine gave a snort. 'Your father is quite capable of looking after himself.'

'I'm not so sure he is.'

'Then he must learn.'

'But he gets so stressed at times over school. He probably wouldn't eat at all and I don't think he can even use the washing machine.'

'Danielle, you cannot be his housekeeper for ever, cooking his meals and clearing up after him. He should not even want that from you. You are a young woman with your whole life ahead of you.'

Alarm bells were ringing in Dani's head as she began to see the difficulties ahead.

'And he's going to be so disappointed when I tell him I'm leaving the bank for the fashion industry of all things — you know he despises it.'

'He will get over it,' Francine said.

Dani tried to calm her fears. Her mum was right. She had to start living her own life.

★　★　★

When Francine left her at the airport, Dani tried to be positive. She'd promised Francine she would be back, that it was the life she wanted. Surely her dad would see what a great opportunity she had been offered. She suspected that might be expecting a lot. Well, she just had to stand firm. Within weeks she could be finished with the bank and back in Paris beginning the new career she had been longing for.

Although she had known Claude for such a short time they had grown close. The feeling she had for him was totally different from the feelings she'd had for Ryan. No matter what her mum had said, Dani wanted to give their relationship time to develop, to find out if she and Claude could have a future together.

There wasn't much chance of that happening if she stayed in Brandwell.

*   *   *

Her dad, Steve, was at the airport to meet Dani and hugged her tight, saying how much he'd missed her and how pleased he was that she was back. He took her case and they chatted happily on the way to the car. Dani felt a warm glow at being home again and eventually began to wonder whether she'd been carried away with all this fashion business and swept of her feet by the attentions of a handsome Frenchman!

Her home was here with her dad. It always had been. She had good friends here. Did she really want to give all this up for an unknown future?

On the motorway heading for home, Steve asked her about Paris.

She tried to answer his questions in as carefree manner as she could without mentioning Claude or the possibility of her move to Paris. She wanted to be absolutely certain before she set the wheels in motion.

Sitting there in the car listening to her dad talking about school and home and what was going on, she wasn't so sure now. However, she'd told her mum she wanted to work with her, and she'd promised Claude she'd be back.

Her insides began to churn as she realised she'd set something in motion that was bound to upset a lot of people, whichever choice she made.

As Steve pulled up outside the house she really didn't know what she wanted or what to do about it.

* * *

Over the next few days Dani tried to find the right moment to discuss with Steve what had transpired in Paris but it proved more difficult than she had expected. He was constantly stressed with school and various changes within the Science department that he didn't agree with. His drawn face and tired eyes worried her and she began to wonder if she really could go off and leave him to cope on his own.

As she settled back at work in the bank, memories of Paris kept forcing their way into her mind. She'd think about the evening with Nancy and the wonderful buzz she'd felt . . . Claude had said he loved her, that he'd wait for her . . . Francine was anxious for her to start working with them as soon as possible.

If it was the life she wanted, then she had to start making it happen.

Doubts kept creeping in. She hardly knew Claude — would he really wait for her? Her mum had warned her to be wary of him, after all. Would she still want to work in Paris if Claude wasn't part of her life?

Her present job might be dull but it was secure. She was doing well, climbing up the ladder. Her boss was encouraging and had nothing but praise for her. She knew she could progress within the system right to the top if she wanted.

Brandwell was home — the only one she had ever known. She was safe here.

★ ★ ★

'Dani, you're back!' Alex squealed when Dani called in at the department store where her friend worked. 'I'm due my break when I've unpacked this box of jackets.'

The two girls had been friends since school days. Alex had found a job straight away while Dani had gone on to college. Now Alex lived with her boyfriend in a small flat, but the girls were still close and saw each other often.

In the canteen they sat with coffees and Alex beamed at her, long blonde hair sweeping her shoulders, blue eyes aglow with anticipation.

'Come on, Dani, tell all. I'm green with envy.'

Dani told her about the places she'd seen, Francine's apartment and her boutiques. Alex sighed wistfully.

'You're so lucky. I'd love to go to Paris. It sounds so romantic.'

When Dani told Alex about the offer Francine had made, Alex stared at her open-mouthed.

'You're going to live in Paris?'

Dani shook her head.

'I don't know . . . I haven't decided yet.'

Alex raised her eyebrows. 'You must be kidding! What's to decide?'

'Alex, it's not that easy. I'm doing well in my present job, and . . . '

'But you hate it. You've been telling me for ages how boring it is.'

'But my dad . . . he'll be on his own and you know what he's like. He'll come home and work on his marking all evening and forget to eat. He's not looking well as it is. I'm worried about him.'

Alex grabbed her hand across the table. 'Dani, you've looked after him for years. You have to think about your own life now.'

Dani sighed. 'I know.'

She didn't mention Claude. Every time she thought about their time together, she had the same warm glow deep within her. Yet some little warning voice inside her head was telling her she should listen to what her mum had told her.

'Have you heard from Ryan?' Alex asked, bringing Dani back from her daydream.

She'd hardly given him a thought

since going to Paris.

'No, not since we split up. Have you seen him? I hope he isn't still moping around.'

'No, he isn't moping. He's seeing Lisa.'

This was the last thing Dani expected. She'd never liked Lisa. She'd been one of the gang who had made her life a misery at school.

'They make a good pair in my book. You're better off without him,' Alex said emphatically.

Dani hadn't expected her ex to replace her so quickly. Yet she had done just that — with Claude.

'Look, I have to get back to work. Adam's out on Tuesdays, so come round later and we can have a proper chat.'

'That would be lovely, Alex. We haven't had one of those for ages.'

Dani knew this would be her chance to mention Claude. Alex would understand, she felt sure of that — and Dani needed someone to share her doubts with.

5

It was three weeks now since Dani had returned from Paris and she still hadn't decided what to do about her job. Every time she was on the verge of handing in her notice, doubts would surface. It seemed such a momentous decision, to leave a career she was progressing well in to start a new life in another country away from all her friends and the home she had always known.

Feeling particularly unsettled after a difficult day at work, she went home tired and dispirited. The house was empty as Steve was at a parents' evening. She kicked off her shoes and looked in the fridge for something she could make a meal out of without cooking.

When the doorbell rang she groaned inwardly. Ryan stood on the doorstep and, fearful of a difficult encounter, she reluctantly asked him in.

He'd smartened himself up: neat haircut, stylish white top and well-cut jeans. He looked fit and muscular. Working with Brad fixing bikes obviously suited him for he seemed more content than usual, smiling smugly as he followed her into the kitchen.

That cheeky look could still stir her feelings and it was odd, thinking that a short time ago she had thought she loved him. Now he was somebody she had known once and grown out of. How could she have changed so quickly? But she hadn't really. The change had been taking place long before she went to Paris.

'Dani, can we talk?' He leaned with his back to the cooker, watching her fill the kettle.

'What about?'

He shook his head and grinned. 'About us, of course.'

She turned to him. 'Ryan, there's nothing to talk about.'

'Oh, but I think there is. I've got a

steady job now, just like you wanted. I'm earning decent money. So, what's the problem?'

'Ryan, I've already told you our relationship is over. We'd been growing apart for ages. I explained how I felt.' She paused and then added, 'And anyway, I've heard you're seeing Lisa.'

He was standing very close now. She knew that look and edged away towards the back door, remembering how his rages could suddenly flare up when someone crossed him.

'Who told you that?'

'It doesn't matter. And I'm pleased for you.'

He stood square in front of her, his expression dark, his voice measured.

'Well, whoever it was doesn't know what they're talking about. Lisa means nothing to me. I took her out a couple of times while you were away, that's all.'

'Ryan, we both have to move on.'

'No, Dani, I am not moving anywhere until you tell me you'll give us another chance.'

His eyes were turning darker, his stance taut and threatening.

She said nothing, knowing from experience how easy it was to ignite that anger. It had frightened her the first time she'd witnessed it, but now she just found it unpleasant, the way his eyes narrowed and his mouth turned into an ugly sneer before the rage broke out.

She'd been grateful when he'd stood up for her at school. It was probably the reason she had allowed their friendship to develop. He'd told her he would always protect her — and nobody messed with Ryan.

Maybe he didn't feel protective now she'd told him she didn't want him any more.

Standing firm, holding onto the unit behind her, she let the kettle boil and turn itself off.

He was fighting for control, almost red in the face. She held his stare, determined not to take her eyes from him, watching him and wishing he would just go away and leave her alone.

Then to her relief he suddenly turned and walked out of the kitchen. She closed and locked the front door firmly as he left, and leaned against the back of it, taking several deep breaths and hoping that was the last she'd see of him.

Eventually she calmed enough to get out her laptop and try to concentrate on the project she was working on. Even though her future with the bank was uncertain, she felt she still had to go through the motions. After half an hour of staring at the screen, nothing had gone in. The encounter with Ryan had unsettled her.

When the doorbell sounded again, Dani tensed. She didn't want another scene.

Relief flooded her when she saw through the glass that it was Meg, the lab technician from her dad's school. Meg was always welcome. She'd been like a second mum to her after Francine had left for France.

'You don't mind a bit of company, do you, Dani?' Meg said, giving her a hug.

'No, I'm glad you came, actually. Dad's out at a parents' evening.'

'Yes, dear, I know. That's why I came. I wanted to talk to you about your dad.'

Meg looked worried and Dani felt herself tense.

They went into the kitchen and Meg eased her large frame onto one of the wooden chairs while Dani got mugs out of the cupboard.

While she waited for the kettle to boil, she turned to Meg. 'So, what's this about Dad?'

Meg moved uncomfortably on her chair. 'Well, I don't want to alarm you . . . ' She hesitated.

Dani's heart began to pound. She knew exactly what was coming.

'I'm worried about him, Dani.'

'It's Zeta, isn't it?'

Meg's kind face took on a troubled look. 'Well, they have been arguing rather a lot lately — and it's getting noticed.'

Dani sighed. She'd heard it all before.

Steve didn't get on with his head of department, had always resented the fact that Zeta had been promoted over him when he was twice her age and reckoned he knew a lot more about teaching than she ever would.

'I knew there was something wrong,' Dani said. 'Dad's been really out of sorts lately, and he looks stressed all the time — I mean even more than normal.'

Meg picked up a spoon from the table and began to turn it over slowly in her hand, not looking at Dani. 'It will probably blow over . . . '

Now Dani was seriously worried.

'What will probably blow over?'

Meg looked up, straight at Dani, and it all suddenly came out in a rush. 'He's been refusing to co-operate with Zeta and it's causing all sorts of tensions within the department — and I'm afraid it's going to get out of hand. There's no reasoning with him, you see.

He's been losing his temper at the least thing.'

She paused and her voice dropped when she added, 'Try and talk to him, Dani. I think he needs help and even if he won't listen to anyone else, he might listen to you.'

'But, Meg, he's always been like this. He and Zeta have never got on.'

'I know, but it's never been as bad as this before. Some of the teachers think he's heading for a breakdown.' She tried to smile but her voice wavered. 'He'll be better now you're back.'

Dani's heart sank. She couldn't leave her dad now. Paris was out of the question. It seemed the decision had been made for her.

Meg sipped her tea then straightened in her chair and seemed to make a big effort at cheering up. 'So how was Paris?'

'Mum's business is doing well.' Dani didn't want to discuss any of it with Meg. There was no point now anyway. All she could think about was whether

her dad was about to have a breakdown and what did that entail and if he did, how would she cope?

When Dani sat down again, Meg took her hand across the table.

'I'm sorry, dear. I didn't mean to upset you. I just thought you ought to know.'

'I'm glad you told me, Meg. I knew something was wrong. But I'm not sure what I can do to help him. You know how stubborn he is. If I try to talk to him about it he'll just say everything's fine and it's nothing to do with me and not to worry.'

Meg sighed. 'I know. I've tried but he won't open up to me. That's why I thought you might be able to get through to him.' Meg's face was full of concern. 'He's such a good teacher and the kids respect him, but he's not very co-operative with the rest of the staff. That's his weakness. I don't suppose either of us will really change him.' She gave Dani a sad smile. 'We both have to look out for him, help him the best we can. That's all we can do.'

'I'll do what I can, Meg. You know I will.'

Meg tried to change the subject by filling her in a bit more about what was going on in school and in Brandwell. When she left, Dani closed the door and sank into the chair in the back room.

Paris and Claude were now out of the question. Her dad needed her.

That evening she emailed Claude rather than talk to him on the phone. That way she could avoid difficult explanations; she couldn't cope with those tonight. Her heart was heavy and she needed time to adjust before she could face telling him she would not be coming back to Paris. Neither could she face telling Francine. Both of them would be shocked and disappointed.

★ ★ ★

Over the next few days Dani tried to come to terms with this new situation, but knowing now that all those possibilities — a career she could only have dreamed of, the man she loved by her side, living with her mum once more — were to be denied her. It made her want all these things even more than ever.

The indecision she had felt had gone. In its place was a desperate desire to be back in Paris with Claude and Francine. It became such an obsession that on her way home one evening she knew she had to do something about it. She had to talk to her dad and tell him how she felt.

He strode into the kitchen that evening as she was peeling potatoes.

'No cooking for you tonight, my love,' he said, taking the knife from her hand. 'We are going out for a meal. You're doing too much — studying for this exam and looking after me too. I wish I could do more to help but the powers that be seem to find a never ending supply of extra work for us teachers these days. Most of it's totally useless, too. If they would just let us get on with teaching, the kids would learn a lot more.'

'I don't mind, Dad. I like cooking, and I really don't feel like going out tonight anyway.'

He looked disappointed but then brightened.

'Of course, you're tired with all this studying. But it will be worth it in the long run. The more qualifications you can get the better. There's nothing more secure than working for a bank. So, if you don't fancy going out, how about a takeaway? You like Chinese.'

'That would be great,' she said, putting the peeled potatoes in a pan of water in the fridge. They'd do for tomorrow.

He seemed relaxed and happy tonight. This might be the perfect time to talk to him. Perhaps the trouble at school had blown over after all. Meg always was a worrier, and Steve had always been like this, difficult to get on with and usually at odds with some member of staff or other. He'd be uptight for a while then, when the trouble was sorted, he'd snap out of it just as quickly.

He was clearly in a good mood tonight, and Dani began to wonder if she dared bring up the subject — she was desperate now to see if going to live in Paris might still be a possibility.

'Will I order, or will you?' he asked.

'Let me. You always order too much rice,' she said, feeling a lift in her spirits. It would be a relief to get it all out in the open.

He let out a chortle. 'OK. I've got marking to do anyway.'

She ordered the Chinese then went up to her bedroom to speak to Claude on the phone. She didn't want to discuss any of the problems with him until she'd sorted it out in her own mind after talking with Steve later, so she tried to keep the conversation light-hearted and asked him about the fashion show and how it was progressing.

However, he must have detected there was something wrong.

'But why have you not given in your notice at the bank yet?' he asked. 'It is weeks since you left Paris. I thought you would have been back here by now.'

'Claude, this is the rest of my life we're talking about. There's no need to rush.'

'But I am impatient to have you here with me again. Do you not feel the same?'

'Yes, of course I want to be with you.'

'But you are not doing anything to make it possible. Do you not care for me any more?'

'You know I do, Claude. Please, just be patient a little longer.'

'Are you sure you've not changed your mind?'

'I can't up and leave at a moment's notice.'

He must have heard the anxiety in her voice and began to reassure her that he would be patient and that she must take as much time as she needed.

When they disconnected, she held the phone close to her heart. Thinking they may never be together was almost unbearable. She had to get back to Paris. She so much wanted to be with him. She had to persuade her dad that this was a good move for her — and she had to persuade herself that her dad could cope without her.

Once she'd composed herself, she went down to join him and wait for the Chinese to arrive

He was in the kitchen pouring himself a beer.

'Dad, I wanted your opinion on something.'

He gave her a questioning look.

'Fire away. Always here to help.'

'You know I've been a bit restless lately . . . '

'Have you?' He looked surprised.

'I've been thinking of changing my career.'

'Whatever for?'

'Because I'm not enjoying my present job.'

'You'll always go through bad patches,' he said, dismissively. 'You just have to struggle on. You'll get past it, move up the scale. When you get to the top you'll be glad you stuck with it.'

His attitude immediately put her on the defensive. He wasn't even listening. He wasn't even going to try to understand how she felt. He was going to be his usual bombastic self.

'But there are no guarantees. I might spend the rest of my life working in the wrong job. I want to change now while I'm still young enough.'

'But you'll never find anything to beat working for a bank. Nice and steady. Good, reliable — '

She interrupted him. 'Mum wants me to go and live in Paris and work with her.'

'Does she now?'

'I thought I might actually be able to discuss it with you.' She couldn't keep the sarcasm from her voice.

He bent down to get dishes out of the cupboard. As he straightened up he shook his head slowly and gave a cynical smile. 'I think it's a crazy idea. Just the sort of thing your mother would come up with. I hope you told her so.'

She took a deep breath

'I'm seriously considering it.'

She closed her eyes waiting for his response. She could feel the tension in his silence.

Then he laughed. 'Your mum always did talk a lot of rubbish. Fancy putting ideas like that into your head!'

Her stomach was in knots but she was determined to stand firm. 'Dad. It's not Mum's decision. It's mine — and I intend to do it.'

He was standing facing her, drinking beer from the can again, not taking her seriously. 'OK, so you've been feeling restless recently, but you don't have to go traipsing off to France. There are plenty of opportunities here for a woman with your qualifications, something that suits you better.'

His attitude was really annoying her now.

'Dad, I *have* found something better. It's working for a big, well established fashion house that's expanding all the time. It's my family's business and I could be part of it, make it even more successful. I'd be using my knowledge and skills and I'd have a secure future. What could be better than that?'

He put on his patient teacher look and his expression softened. 'I despair of your mother at times. You'd be going into a business you know nothing about, and you'd be leaving all this behind. This is your home.'

He'd already picked up a pile of exercise books and was setting himself up at the dining room table for a session of marking. She knew it was pointless to pursue the subject any further so she strode out of the kitchen and went up to her room to phone Alex.

'Dani, calm down. You sound in a right state. He can't make you stay, you know!'

Dani tried to compose herself. 'I know, Alex, and I won't let him, but he won't even listen! He won't even try to understand how I feel. He always thinks he knows best.'

'Dani, you can't turn down the chance of a lifetime just to please your dad. What's he got against it anyway?'

Dani tried to think logically, tried to put herself in his shoes.

'I think he's afraid of me leaving. He's trying to justify it by convincing me — and himself — that it's not a good move for me.'

'You can't stay living with him for ever, though, can you?'

She sighed. Alex always managed to make her feel better. 'I don't think it's that. It's because it's so far away. And he honestly thinks I'm making a big mistake leaving a good, steady job.'

'Why don't you leave it a while and give him time to get used to the idea?'

'But if I'm going to move to France, I have things to sort — and my mum needs to know. I can't just let it drift indefinitely'

'It's Claude, isn't it?' she said, quietly.

Dani could feel the tears pricking her eyes.

'I don't know what to do, Alex. I want to be with Claude, but I do care about Dad.'

'Do you want to come round later for a chat?' Alex asked. 'Adam's out so we'll have the flat to ourselves.'

'Yes, I'd like that,' Dani said in a small voice before she hung up, feeling almost more confused than she had done before she spoke to Alex.

She hadn't felt hungry but she couldn't resist the Chinese when it arrived, it smelled so good.

Her dad seemed to have already forgotten all about their conversation and she knew he'd dismissed it from his mind. It was his way of dealing with difficult subjects.

It was a relief really as she didn't feel up to another row and she didn't want to get him stressed again. Perhaps if she left it a while for him to mull over he might soften and consider what she'd told him.

All she could do was hope.

* * *

Several weeks went by and Steve had still not brought up the subject again. He seemed happier than usual and Dani suspected it was because he thought she had put the matter out of her mind.

Since Dani hadn't told her dad about Claude, for fear of complicating matters, she was always careful not to speak to him over the phone when her dad was within earshot. She and Claude emailed each other every day and this made it easier for her to avoid telling him about the problem she was up against.

Tonight, however, her dad was out and she wanted to hear Claude's voice — but he sounded more subdued than usual.

'Claude, what's the matter?' she

asked after they had exchanged a few words.

'I think you have changed your mind about me,' he said. His voice had lost its warmth and she felt her heart tighten.

Every bit of her wanted to be with him, to see his face, to hold him, to reassure him that her feelings for him had not changed.

'I think if you wanted to be with me, you would be here in Paris by now.' She could hear the catch in his voice.

'I want to be — but I have things I have to deal with. I can't leave just yet.'

'I think you don't know how you feel about me,' he said. 'You have doubts and these are just excuses you tell me.'

'No, that's not it. You know I love you.'

'Then why will you not talk with me when your father is at home, insisting we email only? Do you not want him to know how we feel about each other and how we want to be together? I tell my parents about you. I want them to know you are important to me, and they are happy for me. Will your father not feel the same?'

'He thinks I'm making a mistake by giving up my job here,' she said finally, feeling she could not avoid some sort of explanation any longer.

'But it is your decision, not his.'

'I know, but I have to let him get used to the idea. I don't want to overly upset him.'

'Does he also know you want to be with me?'

'No, not yet . . . '

'I have not spoken with your mother about us. It's for you to tell her, but I do not think she will be against us being together. Why do you insist on keeping it a secret? Are you not sure of your feelings for me?'

'Claude, my dad's still struggling with just the fact that I want to move to Paris.'

'But is your happiness not something he would find pleasing?'

Dani sighed. 'Yes, of course.'

'Then I think that maybe you and your boyfriend are together again.' She could barely hear him.

'Claude, if you think that then we might as well give up now. I have too much on my mind for this sort of conversation.'

There was a silence neither could fill. Then the phone went dead.

Dani sat staring at it. Had he hung up on her?

She phoned him back but was diverted to his voicemail and he didn't return her calls. She emailed him but he didn't answer.

After staring at the screen in numb disbelief for some minutes she rolled her legs over the side of the bed and tried to get up but her legs wouldn't support her. She couldn't stop her hands from shaking and her body felt chilled and fragile.

How had it all gone so wrong so quickly? Claude had said he loved her! He'd said he would be there waiting for her when she got back to Paris. Yet in the span of a phone call everything had changed.

The phone she'd abandoned minutes ago lay on the bed cover. She glanced sideways at it, willing it to ring, but it remained silent. The only noise she could hear was her heart thumping in her chest. Why had he done this to her? What had she said that had made him think she was back with Ryan? How could she have misjudged him so badly when she had thought he really loved her, was so sure his feeling matched hers?

After several long minutes sitting staring at the window, watching the curtains flutter in the breeze, she tried to think more logically and eventually managed to subdue the pain in her heart. If he couldn't try to understand what a big thing this was for her, to move from her home and start afresh in a different country, to leave her dad on his own, then what chance of a future did they have together? And hadn't Francine warned her not to get too close to him? She'd ignored this warning at her peril. Well, at least she knew where she stood now.

* * *

Over the next days she tried hard to dismiss Claude from her mind and concentrate on her plans for the future. Before she had met him she had felt happy, free and optimistic about starting a new career at the bank.

Now she was filled with longings and desires she hardly knew how to handle. She had tried so hard to convince herself it had been an episode of utter madness — and one she had been lucky to escape unscathed.

Could she still work in Paris with her mum and forget all about Claude? But she would relive their time together over and over — how close they had been, his kisses so passionate with promise . . . promise that now seemed to have faded.

Francine's phone calls were always

affectionate but Dani could tell her mum was impatient when she asked her, 'Dani, do you not want to come here and live in Paris?'

'Yes, Mum . . . well, at least, I think so.'

'I don't want to put pressure on you, but if you've decided it's not right, you must tell me.'

'Mum, please give me a little more time.'

Her dad seemed more relaxed than she had ever seen him and she felt sure things had sorted themselves out at school and that he and Zeta had declared a truce.

There seemed no reason now to worry about leaving him.

Yet other doubts troubled her. She still couldn't come to terms with the way Claude had apparently cut her out of his life. Francine had warned her — and now she had to believe it was true. Claude could have his pick of glamorous women. Why would he choose her?

Steve came home earlier than usual one afternoon while Dani was working in the dining room on some files she'd been studying. He sat in the chair by the window and began to chat.

'Do you want me to go upstairs and work?' Dani asked him, knowing he liked to spread his books on the dining table, and she could just as easily lie on her bed and read this stuff.

He shook his head. 'No, I've nothing to do this evening. I wondered if you fancied a walk. It's lovely out in the woods at this time of year.'

She stared at him. He never came home from school without a pile of marking to do and lessons to prepare.

'No, Dad, I've a lot to get through before morning. You go, though. Do you good.'

He got up and stretched. 'I think I will.'

Once he'd left the house Dani wondered at the change in him. It was three weeks until the end of term and that was usually a stressful time for him with exams and reports to write.

As the next few days went by, he spent most of his evenings watching television. When Dani commented on it he told her he'd managed to do all his school work in free lessons and at lunch time. She was pleased to see him so much more relaxed and didn't question him further.

He hadn't complained about anything lately, and she hadn't heard anything more from Meg. On the surface all seemed well — yet there was something strangely worrying about it.

Occasionally she sent an email to Claude although she really didn't expect a reply, yet she couldn't resist just once in a while in the forlorn hope he might respond. He never did.

There was no point in bringing the subject of Claude up with Francine because Dani knew what her advice would be.

Following a long phone call with

Francine one evening, Dani's mind was troubled. There had been a lack of the warmth she usually felt when talking to her mum and she was afraid Francine was losing patience with her.

Maybe this would be a good time to take the two weeks holiday she was still due and go and see her mum again. She made an impromptu decision. First thing on Monday morning, she would see if she could book the two weeks at short notice.

After making this decision she felt energised and spent Saturday cleaning the house from top to bottom. If she stocked up the freezer, her dad could cope for the couple of weeks' holiday.

Yet Claude was constantly on her mind. What was he doing? Who was he with? Why was he acting so strangely?

Then Francine's warnings would ring in her ears. He'd obviously found someone else. He could never have really loved her. She had to force herself to accept this. Yet some little nugget of hope lingered in her heart. She had to know. She had to have one more try.

Her dad was out, so she had the house to herself. She picked up the house phone, one she had never rung Claude on before. He wouldn't recognise the number, so he might answer it.

He did.

'Dani!' There was confusion and disbelief in his voice.

She was at a loss how to proceed now that she had him on the other end of the line. Panic seized her. She hadn't thought it through.

There was a long silence then a voice she recognised echoed in the background.

It was Rêve. They were together.

She should have known!

Without another word she hung up the call.

She sat in the fading light of evening, the phone clutched to her chest. She squeezed her eyes tight and tried to think logically.

Why shouldn't he be with her? They worked together, didn't they? But try as she might, she could not rid her mind of the picture of them together.

Why had she been so stupid? She had known all along that Rêve was more his type, glamorous and sophisticated. Of course he would be with Rêve. It was why he hadn't responded to her emails. Why had she put herself through all this again when she should have known?

By Sunday evening, she knew she had to see her mum and nothing was going to stop her. Claude could do what he liked from now on and it would be no concern of hers.

Steve was watching a nature programme on TV and when it finished he got up and turned it off and said he was going out.

'Dad, before you disappear again, I want to ask you something.'

'Go ahead,' he said, stretching lazily.

'I'd like to go to Paris again — just for a couple of weeks to see Mum.'

He looked surprised then shrugged. 'Good idea. You need a holiday. You've been looking a bit peaky lately. When are you going?'

'I've a couple of weeks holiday left but I haven't booked it yet.'

'Then get on to them first thing in the morning. Tell them you need a break after all this studying.'

She was surprised at his reaction.

'Off you go. I don't want you moping around here cleaning up after me. I'm quite capable of doing all that myself, you know. Go off to Paris for a couple of weeks — do you loads of good.'

'Are you sure you'll be all right?'

'Of course I will. Whatever made you think I can't cope without you?'

As he pulled on his coat and left the house Dani shook her head in disbelief. He was happy about her going.

Well, she wasn't going to argue with that. She'd see her mum again — and she wasn't even going to think about Claude.

6

While doing some last-minute shopping in Brandwell before flying to Paris, Dani bumped into Ryan's mum.

Marianne's head was bowed and she nearly collided with Dani. When she looked up Dani was shocked at how awful she appeared, her pretty blonde hair straggling around her pale face, her eyes heavy and red-rimmed. Dani had always been fond of Marianne, a small, gentle woman, and she felt a pang of regret that now their relationship was different.

It took Marianne a minute to register who she was. Then she smiled.

'Dani, good to see you.' The two women hugged, then Marianne's face clouded. 'I don't suppose you've heard from Ryan?'

'No, not recently.'

Marianne looked distraught. 'I'm so

worried about him. He hasn't been home for a couple of weeks and he's not answering his mobile.'

Dani hesitated before saying, 'You know we've split up, don't you?'

Marianne sighed. 'Yes, he told me.'

'We were already growing apart, Marianne. It wouldn't have worked.'

Marianne gave a wan smile.

'I suppose I always knew that. But he did love you in his own way, Dani. He was different when he was with you. I really began to believe he'd left all his bad ways behind him.'

'I'm sorry.'

'He hasn't been in to work either,' Marianne continued. 'Brad's angry and says he's got lots of bikes in for repair and Ryan's let him down. I doubt he'll take him back when he does bother to appear.'

She looked at Dani, anxious and tearful.

'If you do hear from him, you will let me know, won't you?'

'Of course. But try not to worry.

Ryan knows how to look after himself. And Alex told me she's seen him around with Lisa. In fact, why don't you try her flat?'

Marianne shook her head. 'I did, but she said she didn't know anything. She's trouble, that one. What chance does he stand now he's hitched up with her? I really despair of him!'

Dani could see the despair in her whole demeanour, but then Marianne seemed to brighten suddenly.

'Maybe he'll get in touch with you. He always respected you, Dani. If he was in trouble, you'd probably be the person he'd turn to. You've been friends a long time. Try and talk to him, will you?'

Dani didn't have the heart to tell her she was off to Paris and was unlikely to see Ryan again anyway.

Later, when her dad came home Dani told him she'd seen Marianne and that Ryan was missing.

'She asked if I knew where he was,' she said.

'And do you?' Steve asked sharply.

'Dad, I already told you we're finished.'

'Well, I'm glad to hear it. Nothing but trouble, that lad. He was the bane of my life at school and from what I hear, he hasn't changed one bit. You keep away from him.'

Dani was ready to snap back, but stopped herself. He'd been relaxed and cheerful over the past few days and she didn't want to do anything to upset him again.

'I feel sorry for Marianne, though. It's not her fault the way he behaves, is it?' she said.

Steve took a softer tack.

'Maybe I'll go round and have a word with her.'

'Oh, Dad, that would be great. I know she'll really appreciate it. She knows how you tried to help him at school.'

'Well, I did my best, but there's no helping some lads. They seem to be born bad.'

'You will go round and see her, won't you? She's all on her own and she doesn't know which way to turn. And she was always kind to me.'

'Don't worry, love. I always liked her, too.'

★   ★   ★

Next day Steve told Dani he'd made enquiries with some lads Ryan hung out with but no one would admit to knowing where he was.

He also told her he'd been to see Marianne and had promised her he would keep his ear to the ground for any information on his whereabouts.

It played on Dani's mind as she started to pack. She wished she could have reassured Marianne that Ryan was all right before she left.

Maybe he would answer her call, even if he wasn't responding to his mother. Nervously, she dialled the number.

He answered immediately.

'Ryan, where are you? Your mum's really worried. And Brad's not too pleased either.'

There was a pause.

'Dani, I need to see you. Can you get away, meet me in the park?'

She hesitated. But it was the only way she could find out what he was up to and put Marianne's mind at rest.

As she walked across the fields, her anxiety grew. What did he want? Maybe she should have phoned Marianne and told her where he was. But she'd be at work now and wouldn't be able to get there. No, she had to do this herself.

The park was deserted except for a lone dog walker the other side of the playing field. Ryan was standing beside his motorbike under a clump of trees near the entrance, his usual cocky self, yet handsome with it. His dark eyes fixed on her and she tried to avoid looking into them. They reminded her of times when those eyes had stirred such passion in her that she had been unable to see his faults.

As he approached her she backed away.

'Dani, what's wrong with you? You look like a frightened kitten. I only want to talk.'

'What do you want to talk about?'

Again he approached and this time she stood her ground.

He was facing her, feet astride, head held high.

'I want us to get back together again.'

She sighed. 'Ryan, I already told you that isn't going to happen. You know it isn't.'

'Why not? We got on well together all those years. What's changed?' His voice had taken on a softer tone. He'd always known how to put on the charm.

'*I've* changed,' she murmured.

'So have I.' He moved closer and put his hands on her shoulders. Their eyes met. 'You're my girl, Dani. There's no other girl for me.'

'You're seeing Lisa — and I'm pleased for you.'

His grip tightened and his face took on a harder look. 'I've told you she means nothing to me.'

Dani tried to stand firm, hold his gaze.

'Ryan, I'm going to Paris to live with my mum.'

Although she had her doubts as to whether this would actually happen it seemed a good way of making him accept that there was no way they were ever going to get together again.

She could see anger building in him.

'I'm pleased you've got Lisa. Just don't let her get you into trouble again,' she said.

'You're not listening to me, Dani. I don't want her. I want you. And you want me, don't you? Otherwise why are you here?'

Dani felt her own anger rising to meet his. What right did he have to bully her like this? And to treat his mother in this way? She wrenched his hands from her shoulders.

'I'm here because your mum's worried sick. She says you haven't been home for weeks. What are you up to, Ryan?'

He shrugged. 'This and that.'

She could guess what that meant.

'Ryan, why don't you ever think of

anyone but yourself? Your mother's in pieces worrying about you. You must let her know where you are and go and see Brad and make your peace with him.'

'What for?'

'Because it's the first real job you've had. And you're good at it. Nobody can take a motorbike to pieces and fix it the way you can. Brad appreciates that. Why waste all that?'

'Like you're going to, you mean?'

It silenced her for a moment.

'It's different,' she said quietly.

'No, it isn't. You're giving up on us — on your job. What's different?'

'I've got something to take its place.'

Not taking his eyes from her, he said slowly, 'I've got something to take its place, too. It's called living by your wits. Why slave for Brad when I can get by fine without any of that bother?'

'Ryan, please don't go down that route again. You were doing so well.'

His expression suddenly lightened and he completely changed direction.

'OK, Dani, I accept what you're

telling me. Can we still be friends?'

She smiled with relief. He was being reasonable and not going to make a scene! She was used to these shifts in his mood, and this time felt it could work to her advantage. He'd taken on board what she'd said and maybe he'd go and see Brad, and she could reassure Marianne she'd seen him.

'Of course we can be friends. We've known each other a long time and I still worry about you.'

'No need. I'm doing fine.'

He walked over to his motorbike then glanced back at her with that mischievous smile that had won her heart so many times.

'Fancy a spin?'

She remembered that first time she'd gone on the back of his bike, all those years ago when they were still at school. He was too young then to even be riding a motorbike.

Her resolve was weakening. Should she succumb to his charm just once more, as a show of friendship? She didn't want to hurt him more than necessary and in his present mood she could still feel a tenderness for him.

'OK, but don't go tearing round like a lunatic.'

Grinning, he handed her the spare helmet and she tucked her hair in as best she could. Then she hopped on the back while he revved up.

They took the path out of the park and began to pick up speed as the road led out into open countryside. She clung on round his waist feeling the exhilaration of the wind in her face as if she was sixteen again, knowing that if her dad ever found out he'd go berserk. On one occasion he had, and she'd been grounded for a week!

After several miles Ryan stopped the bike in a lay-by and she hopped off. They scrambled down the bank beside the canal as they had done so many times in the past. She'd always loved it down here. It was so peaceful. The sun was warm with a gentle breeze freshening the air, rolling countryside stretching out before her. Could she leave all this behind?

She faced Ryan and saw he'd removed his helmet and was again looking serious.

'Dani, please don't go. Let's at least give it one more try.'

His eyes were pleading and she felt her resolve weakening. It would be so easy to slip into her old life, to care for her dad, to stick with the bank, to see Alex for girlie chats — and to carry on going out with Ryan.

At least he seemed to want her, not like Claude who wouldn't even speak to her now. Love wasn't what she'd thought it would be. But deep inside she knew she wouldn't find it with Ryan.

'Ryan, I can't!'

He grabbed her arm and as she twisted to free herself he caught her and drew her closer to him. The feel of his firm body brought back more tender feelings, memories of times when those strong arms had comforted and protected her. It was like coming home. Familiar and safe.

But it wasn't safe! Ryan was never safe. Even now, she didn't know what he was up to. She wrenched herself free.

A narrow boat glided by and the skipper gave them a friendly wave.

'Want a ride in one?' Ryan asked her, cocking his head to one side, again with that cheeky grin on his face. He never really took anything seriously for long. 'I could get into one of those things easily.'

'No, Ryan!' she snapped.

'There's no pleasing you sometimes.'

'Ryan, it's over between us. Why can't you understand that?'

He came towards her, hurt twisting his face into bitterness.

'Because I stuck at that job at Brad's for *you*.' He was very close now. 'Dani, I've never felt about anyone the way I do about you.'

She backed away and he stopped her, grabbing her shoulders. She tried to push past him but was in no way equal to his strength. He gripped her shoulders and turned her to face him.

'Dani, I swear to you that Lisa means nothing to me. It's you I want.'

'Ryan, you won't achieve anything by this. Now, can we please go back? I'm going to Paris in two days' time and I still have a lot to do.'

The gentle touch of her hand on his arm brought a look of tenderness to his face. He slipped his arms round her and she didn't resist as he gave her a hug. Then he stepped back, defeated, and her heart twisted with pain.

They got back on the bike and he dropped her off at the end of her road.

She didn't go home. Instead she made her way back to the park. She needed space and solitude to think things out, work out what was happening.

⋆ ⋆ ⋆

Two days later Dani was back with her mum in Paris. As Francine drove out of the airport she told her they were going straight to her grandparents' house where she would stay for a few days.

'I think Lou and Nico will want to see you. It's a long time since you visited them,' Francine said.

'But, Mum, I want to spend my time in Paris with you.'

'And I want you with me in Paris,' Francine said. 'There's much work to be done. But I want you to tell me whether you are still thinking about coming to work with me here — or not.'

'Mum, I'm sorry I've been dithering over it. Dad's not been well and I was worried about him. But he seems better now.'

'I fear your father does not approve of this move and is making it difficult for you.'

'You seemed angry last time we spoke.'

'My dear, I was angry with him, not you. I'm sorry if it appeared that way.' Francine turned to give her an affectionate smile. 'I know it's a big decision for you, but you must make that decision for yourself, not your father.'

'And I will, Mum. Dad likes to have his say but he wouldn't stop me from doing something I really want to do.'

'That's good, then. I think maybe this holiday will help you decide. But first, your grandparents want to see you and spoil you a little. It's Nico's birthday tomorrow and there's to be a dinner party with family and friends. I don't think you would want to miss that.'

'Of course not, Mum.'

Dani felt easier in her mind now she'd talked with Francine, and a few days with Lou and Nico would be a welcome break — a little time without any pressures.

As they sped along in the car she settled back in her seat and tried hard to focus on the two weeks ahead and keep all thoughts of Claude from her mind. She couldn't even bring herself to say his name for fear of being told what in her heart she already knew

— that he was now with Rêve or some other woman and had forgotten all about her. She hoped Francine wouldn't bring him into their conversation.

If she did come to work in Paris, then she would have to face up to seeing him from time to time. But first she had to focus her mind on her career and whether she really did want to make such a big change in her life.

★　★　★

Looking out of the bedroom window next morning across rolling country-side, Dani knew a peace she hadn't felt for months. She had always loved this old farmhouse where her grandparents, Lou and Nico, lived. The magnificent big rooms with their dark furnishings were full of childhood memories. She had rarely visited them in France in recent years. There had always seemed so much to do in the holidays and, during term time, it had been impossible once the pressure of exams began.

Last night she had revelled in the joy of being with them again and, after a long soak and a delicious meal she had been happy to collapse into the huge bed under a soft duvet.

She ambled downstairs in her pyjamas, yawning and stretching, to find Lou in the big farmhouse kitchen peeling apples for pies.

'Your grandfather has just brought these in from our store from last autumn,' Lou said. 'My apple pies are always a favourite when we have these dinners.'

'I'm really looking forward to seeing all the aunts and uncles again,' Dani said.

'And they will want to see you, too. It's many years now since we had a family gathering with you here too.' Lou dried her hands and took a crusty loaf from the cupboard. 'But now you're ready for breakfast, I think.'

Dani sat at the scrubbed oak table. 'I'm always hungry when I'm here,' she said.

Lou studied her. 'That is good. I think you need this holiday.'

'Where's Mum?' she asked, then remembered she'd said she had to visit one of their suppliers.

'Your mother had business to attend to but she will be back later for the celebration,' Lou assured her. 'She is to drive back with Claude. You have met Claude, I think. He is a very special person. Your grandfather would not have his party without him being here.'

Dani froze. This could be the most awful evening of her life! What if he brought Rêve? Or one of the other models? She didn't think she could bear it. To have to sit through the whole dinner and then spend the rest of the evening in his company would be torture.

She'd thought she was safe here for a few days before she had to face him. She knew it would be inevitable if she came to work in Paris, but at least in the workplace she could be aloof and businesslike about it. Now it was going to be in the midst of her family and possibly friends she didn't even know.

Dani was in a state of anxiety all day as she helped Lou with the preparations for the dinner party, not knowing whether she wanted the time to rush by and get it over with or stand still to delay the moment when she would see him again.

Would he be pleasant or completely ignore her? Would she still feel the same about him? So much had happened since they'd last been together. Had he ever really felt what she thought he had felt?

When everything was complete Lou told Dani to go for a wander round the garden.

'You look pale, my dear. Some fresh air will do you good, bring the roses back into your cheeks.'

As Dani walked round the garden, her nerves began to calm. What would be would be, and there was no point driving herself into a state over it.

By four o'clock she couldn't keep her

eyes off the driveway.

At five she found Nico tending his beans in the vegetable garden. He told her not to fret, that Claude was picking Francine up from a meeting and they had been delayed a little.

He smiled indulgently when he saw her frown.

'They will be here soon. Now you go and get some rest. We have a long evening ahead.'

By six they still had not arrived.

'You must get ready for dinner, now, Dani,' Lou told her. 'We do not want out guests to meet you in the kitchen.'

She went up to the bedroom in a state of nervous tension. Helping Lou with the last-minute preparations had taken her mind off it. Now, on her own, she couldn't control her shaking hands and her legs felt weak and wobbly.

She pulled on the green silk dress Francine had bought for her. The delicate material slid down over her slim hips and she enjoyed a sensuous delight in the smoothness of it. The emerald choker, a gift from Lou, set off the whole outfit. If only Dad could see her!

A frown clouded her face. He wouldn't be impressed.

But Claude would.

The thought sent a tremble of anxiety through her. She tried to fix her hair up in a more sophisticated style but her hands were shaking and bits kept falling out of the clips, so she let it all out to fall loose around her shoulders.

It seemed to her as if she had no control over anything any more!

The guests began to arrive.

The uncles and aunts were a noisy lot, all talking together, and her heart warmed at the memory of these get-togethers years ago when she was just a child. She wanted to see them again — but she didn't want Claude to be there.

Part of her wanted to stay in the safety of her bedroom but she knew she couldn't do that. She took a deep breath, took one last look in the mirror, dabbed on some perfume and walked downstairs, willing her legs to stay firm.

7

Voices and laughter filtered up from the library where the family had gathered. It was a large room furnished in heavy mahogany from floor to ceiling, where leather-bound volumes intermingled with priceless antiques.

Dani stood nervously at the open door. The women were seated in comfortable leather chairs while the men stood in a group, ruby wine shining from crystal goblets.

As soon as she entered, all eyes turned to Dani but she saw only one pair. They were holding her in their deep, dark gaze.

'My, you do look beautiful, my little English princess,' Nico was saying as he drew her into their circle and introduced her to his friends.

She was aware that Claude's eyes never left her as she answered their questions confidently, her French coping easily with the situation.

'I hear you may be joining the business,' Marcel, a friend of Nico's, said.

'I hope so,' she replied, then glanced at her mother and saw the same concerned look on her face she had glimpsed yesterday in the car. Her heart contracted. Maybe Claude's look had meant nothing. He was always charming to everyone. Maybe Francine could sense danger, maybe even knew what Dani suspected — that he and Rêve were together.

Marcel broke into her thoughts. 'Well, you have every advantage — a successful mother, an influential grandfather.'

Nico stopped him mid-sentence. 'No, no, that is not the case, Marcel. Francine insists she has no advantage. She will learn like all other employees. She will start at the bottom and work her way up.'

'She will not be very long in getting

to the top, I think. An intelligent and beautiful young woman, and with such elegance.' He looked at her and smiled indulgently. 'If they don't treat you well, my dear, you come and work for me. I will have you modelling my collection.'

Marcel took her arm to lead her into dinner.

A great surge of relief flooded her as she realised she was not going to be sitting beside Claude. She could focus on her family during the meal and would not have to make polite conversation with him.

That one glance into his familiar face had rekindled all sorts of desires within her and she was struggling to keep them under control.

Marcel pulled out the chair for her to sit, then took his place beside her. The meal was served in the splendid dining room by two elderly women who had been hired for the occasion.

Dani was monopolised throughout the meal by her two aunts who wanted to catch up on all the details of her life for the past ten years and whom she willingly obliged.

It was not until much later in the evening when most of the guests had left that Dani felt she could escape to the solitude of her room. She knew she wouldn't be able to cope with any polite conversation with Claude, and she hoped that by the time she got up in the morning he would have left the house.

However, as she reached the turn of the stairs she heard footsteps and knew instinctively he was behind her.

'Dani, I would like us to talk for a while. Will you join me for a nightcap before you disappear to your bed?'

He took her arm and, not trusting her voice, she silently turned and let him lead her back towards the library.

As soon as they were inside with the door shut he let go of her arm and stood facing her. She stood mutely staring at the floor, unable to meet his gaze until he lifted her chin and she was forced to look into his eyes. They were troubled, his mouth a tight line.

'Dani, it's good to see you,' he said softly.

She knew she should be strong and tell him what she thought of him. He had treated her like all his other women and she didn't trust him. But her heart was beating fast and she was finding it difficult to breathe.

He waited for her to speak and when she remained silent he gently touched her arm. She flinched and pulled away, her whole body beginning to tremble.

He let his arm drop. 'Dani, talk to me.'

If only she could find her voice or even walk out of the room, but his presence had affected her deeply and she could think of nothing to say.

Still he kept his eyes on her. 'Please . . . '

Finally she managed to form the words, careful to keep her voice as steady as possible.

'Claude, there is nothing I want to talk to you about. You made it very clear that you no longer care for me.'

He took a sharp intake of breath.

'Dani, I have never stopped caring for you.' His voice was low and measured.

Her chin began to tremble and her heart grew tight. All her senses were responding to this man. He still loved her — he still cared for her!

He moved towards her and took both her hands in his. 'I am so sorry you thought that of me.'

The mutual attraction was crackling in the air between them and when he opened his arms for her, she fell into them, knowing at that moment she was lost.

His kiss was unbearably tender and filled with unspoken longing. The world receded, all her problems vanished and all that mattered was that they were together again.

When he finally let her go Dani collapsed into one of the large arm-chairs in the book-lined room.

Claude moved to stand in front of the fireplace and took a sip of his brandy, unable to take his eyes from her.

'Claude, it's so hot in here. Could we go out into the garden for a little while?'

He was quick to observe the unnaturally high colour in her cheeks and the slight unsteadiness of her eyes. He gently pulled her to her feet and, supporting her firmly, led her out through the French doors and onto the terrace.

The night air was cool. An owl could be heard some distance away. A crescent moon rested in a black velvet sky.

'A little too much wine,' he told her as they walked into the rose garden.

'I'm sorry,' she said in a small voice.

'It is nothing. A little fresh air and you will feel better.'

As she walked round the gravel path, her head comfortably resting on Claude's shoulder, his arm tightened round her waist possessively and she relaxed against him, safe in his love.

He turned to her. 'Dani, I have to tell you . . . '

She put a finger to his lips. 'Not now, Claude. I don't want anything to spoil this evening.'

His face relaxed into a smile. 'Tomorrow, then, we will talk.'

★   ★   ★

The next morning her head ached and one look in the mirror did nothing to make her feel better. Claude and Francine had left after an early breakfast and would not be back before late afternoon, so she had most of the day to explore the gardens and woods surrounding this beautiful old house.

It seemed she was the only person in the house. Nico had said he would be busy with preparations for the local carnival. Downstairs all trace of the party had been cleared away and there was warm bread and coffee waiting for her in the kitchen.

After two cups of the fragrantly strong brew she felt better and wandered out into the same garden she had walked with Claude last night.

Then she remembered.

What was it he had to tell her?

Last night it seemed he was sorry for the way he had treated her, but it could be anything. It could be . . .

No, she wasn't going to think about it. It was too painful. She'd wait until he came back and then they would talk. But her happiness had evaporated and she knew she would spend the rest of the day in dread of what might come.

Last night it had felt as if they had never been apart. He'd said nothing about their last phone call, or the long gap of silence that had followed. He hadn't brought anyone to the party except Francine — but that didn't mean there wasn't someone. Good manners would have prevented him from bringing a guest to the house who was likely to upset the family. Rêve still hovered at the back of Dani's mind.

In the library Claude's kiss had been full of passion, but it didn't mean he loved her or had waited for her. After all, she remembered how he had held Rêve in his arms to comfort her and then told Dani there was nothing between them. Francine's words kept repeating in her mind. She'd told her Claude loved all the ladies. She shouldn't have jumped to conclusions so readily last night.

These thoughts wouldn't leave her as she walked in the warm sun and breathed the heavy rose perfume. Wandering through a small gate at the far end of the rose garden and along a gravel path she remembered led to the stables, she wondered if Nico still had Snowy, the lovely white mare she had nicknamed as a child. And Louis, the black stallion who had always terrified her by his size and strength. Suddenly she had to have the feel of Snowy beneath her, the exhilaration of galloping across the fields, something that would rid her mind of these tortured thoughts.

Both horses were being led across the yard when she arrived. Nico greeted her warmly, and the elderly groom made a great fuss at seeing her again.

'You must ride later this afternoon,

Dani. It is much too hot now in this midday sun,' Nico said.

'Nico, please let me ride now. I need to clear my head after last night.'

'Then you should be resting. I will walk back to the house with you.' He turned to the groom and gave his instructions. 'Come, my dear, we will have Snowy ready for you at four o'clock.'

There was no arguing with Nico and she knew it was sensible anyway.

'I'll sit in the orchard, then, and read. It's shady there and I don't feel like sleeping again. I've only just got up.'

He smiled at her indulgently.

'You must do whatever you please. But you must forgive me if I take my usual nap. I'm afraid I'm too old to begin new habits.'

He kissed her and strode purposefully back towards the house.

★ ★ ★

She thought it was part of her dream when she woke and saw Claude hovering above her holding the two horses by their bridles and giving her an amused smile.

'Come on, sleepy head. Do I have to wait all day for my ride?'

She rubbed her eyes and tried to convince herself it was real.

'I have worked six hours, driven half way across France to be with you, and still you sleep!'

She pulled herself up from beneath the apple tree where she had fallen asleep and ran her fingers through her tousled hair.

'Perhaps you do not feel like riding?'

She heard the concern in his voice and wondered if she really looked that rough.

'Yes, yes, I do. I'm sorry. I just drank too much last night and slept too little.'

He tied the horses to a tree and came towards her. 'There's no hurry. We can talk a while. It's still very hot.'

He lowered himself to the ground beside her and took her hand. Despite her resolve, happiness swelled inside her.

'Dani, we need to talk.'

The flurry of excitement she had felt was crushed instantly as she wondered what was coming. She remembered how gentle he had been with Rêve when he was telling her that he loved Dani. Maybe he was about to put her straight too.

Her whole body turned rigid as she tried desperately to stop the shaking that had suddenly convulsed her.

'Claude, I'm sorry. I had things to deal with at home. I didn't mean to mess you about.'

He turned and troubled brown eyes met hers. 'What is this thing you have to deal with?'

'I tried to tell you, but . . . ' She couldn't continue.

'Please, go on. What is it you are trying to tell me?' he said, anxiety distorting his features.

'It's a lot of things. My dad, my job . . . '

He squeezed her hand so tight it hurt. 'And?'

'Nothing else.'

'Not your boyfriend, Ryan?'

'No, I told you. We're finished.'

She was torn between anguish and guilt and a whole lot of other emotions she had been doing her best to ignore. But one thing she was certain of — now that she had spent time with Claude again and confirmed her strong feelings for him she knew that, whatever the outcome of this talk, there could never be anyone else.

Claude let out the breath he'd been holding.

'Dani, I'm sorry. I didn't understand. I felt sure you had changed your mind — about us.'

Suddenly he stood and pulled her to her feet. He gripped her shoulders and the intensity of his look almost alarmed her.

'I thought you had gone back to your boyfriend and that was why you sounded so distant, not warm and loving as you were the last time we were in Paris. And I just couldn't talk any more. I was too upset.'

She looked up into his troubled face. 'Claude, there is no one else. I love you.' His grip loosened and his features relaxed. 'But, what about you? Do you have someone else?' Fear coursed through her as she waited for his reply.

'There is nobody but you, my darling.'

Waves of relief rolled over her as he gathered her close and, in the circle of his arms, she felt the love she had doubted. When finally they drew apart they were both smiling.

Then he was suddenly serious again.

'But what is this worry about your father? This is why you have not finished with your bank and come to Paris to work?'

Dani tensed. She knew she couldn't keep her concerns away from him any longer.

'My dad's not been well. He suffers from stress, and there was some trouble at school. I felt I couldn't leave him just then. But he's better now, so all being well I'll be able to make my plans soon.'

He pulled her to him again and whispered into her hair. 'I understand. I will be patient. So long as one day we can be together. That's all I want.'

'I promise we will,' she said. And she meant it.

Suddenly feeling elated, she turned to the horses and cried out, 'Come on, I'll race you to the top of the hill.'

Before he had realised what was happening she had swung herself into the saddle and had Snowy turned towards the gate.

He quickly took up her challenge and was soon following her out of the field and up the steep lane on the majestic Louis. He kept a steady canter behind her as she spurred the white horse on, a slight recklessness in her seat. Smiling to himself he thought she was the most incredible woman he had ever known.

Finally she slowed by the entrance to the wood and he drew alongside her. She was flushed and breathless as she sat there in the saddle smiling in triumph.

'You ride well,' he said as he swung himself out of the saddle.

He held Snowy for her to dismount and steadied her with his other hand.

Then his arms slipped round her waist and he drew her to him. Their bodies came together and his eyes were full of passion as their mouths touched. Her whole body was alive and reacting to his kiss, his touch, the smell and feel of him until there was nothing else except this moment with this man.

★   ★   ★

That evening Francine sprang a surprise on Dani. They were sitting down to dinner round the big table in the farmhouse kitchen, drinking wine and laughing about events of the day, when Claude stood up and prepared to leave.

'I don't want to interrupt this very pleasant evening but it's time for me to go back. I have to be at a photoshoot first thing in the morning.'

Francine raised a hand to stop him.

'Not so fast, Claude,' she said. 'I've arranged everything. I'll go back early in the morning and deal with the photographer, so you can stay here and look after Dani.'

He raised an eyebrow. 'But you told me I was to look after this so that *you* can spend time here with your daughter.'

'That was the plan, but I can't keep up with her! You're young and I think she will not mind if we make this change. That's if you don't mind?'

Dani looked at Claude and they both knew the arrangement would suit them just fine.

'Francine, you are very kind and I would be honoured to take care of Dani. I could stay with my parents as they do not live so far away.'

Nico coughed. 'Now, Claude, you must do as you wish, but you are more than welcome to stay here with us. We have a very large house and one more guest will hardly cause a problem.'

Claude nodded. He seemed bemused

by this turn of events. Then he looked at Francine.

'Are you sure you don't need me? This will put a lot of extra work on your shoulders.'

She waved dismissively. 'I shall be pleased to have some peace and quiet. You work too hard, Claude, and you deserve a break.'

Dani's insides were churning. She was to have Claude all to herself. He would take her everywhere, just as he had in Paris.

'You're happy with this arrangement, Dani?'

'Of course, Mum, thank you.'

Dani could hardly contain her excitement. Yet she was a little puzzled at Francine letting them to spend time together when previously she had warned her not to get involved with Claude. Perhaps she had seen how happy they were and had decided maybe it would all turn out well.

★　★　★

Next morning Dani was careful to look her best when she went down to breakfast, thinking that Claude would be there, but he was already out with Nico.

'They are talking shop,' Lou said with a tut.

Dani was quite relieved that she could breakfast alone. The day ahead with Claude promised much, so a little anticipation was delicious.

Lou was making her favourite — French toast with lots of honey dribbled over it. When Lou put the plate in front of her she attacked it with her knife and fork as if she hadn't eaten for a week.

Lou looked on approvingly. 'That's better. I think now you are happy and will eat properly.'

Why were they always trying to fatten her up? At home she was the envy of her friends. Alex was always moaning that Dani could eat what she liked and never get fat. Not that Alex was fat. Dani thought she had a better figure than hers with a few more curves. Although at this rate she would be acquiring more curves than she wanted!

The back door opened and Nico and Claude came into the kitchen.

'Ah, I see you have decided to get up.' Claude laughed when he saw her.

'It's only ten o'clock and I'm on holiday.'

'Well, we have much to see today so you must eat up and we will make a start. Your mother has given me a challenging task!'

'Now, don't rush her,' Lou retorted. 'I have made a special breakfast for her and she will not be hurried.'

Dani grinned and made a point of pouring a second cup of coffee. Claude smiled good-naturedly. 'I have no chance of winning, I see.' So he sat down and picked up the coffee pot.

★　★　★

Soon they were in Claude's car speeding along quiet country lanes.

'Where are we going?' Dani asked him.

158

'First I will take you to my village to meet my parents,' he told her. 'It's a pretty village and I think you'll like it. This area is not like Paris. There are no important places to see. But the countryside is pleasant.'

Panic engulfed her. Meeting his parents? She wasn't expecting this — she wasn't ready for it!

'You don't want to meet them?' He glanced sideways at her, quick to pick up her reluctance.

'I don't know . . . ' she said, then realised she'd upset him. 'Well, yes, of course I do. It's just . . . well, a bit of a surprise, that's all. I'd love to meet them. After all, you've met most of my family.'

'Except your father. I think he is important in your life.' His focus was on the road now, his voice more measured.

She felt her throat tighten. She hadn't thought about her dad since arriving back in France and it gave her a guilty jolt. Claude glanced at her.

'Yes, he is,' she said and he left it at that.

It was a tiny hamlet rather than a village, with a few stone houses well off the main road. They parked the car at the end and walked hand in hand down a rough, unmade track to a small cottage.

Filipe and Elise Duval spoke no English and so they were very relieved when Dani spoke to them in French.

'I told you she is as French as you and me and that you had nothing to worry about,' Claude teased his mother good-naturedly.

Elise was a homely little woman and Dani loved her as soon as she saw her. Filipe was more reserved and kept very much in the background. They sat by the open window with a view over fields and woods.

'It's very quiet,' Dani said.

Elise chuckled. 'Ah, not so much. Next door we have Noel and he makes all sorts of ironwork — gates, garden lights. Then there is Florence, she has many cats — very smelly! Also Jean-Pierre breeds dogs and they bark sometimes for hours. And on the way in you passed the Revyes household. Did you see the gîte? All summer long there are holiday makers with their children. French rural life is not very quiet, I think!'

'But you wouldn't live anywhere else, would you?' Claude said.

'I would not like to live in a city. Your mother is very brave living in Paris, Dani. How does she cope with all the traffic and the people?'

'My mum is just the opposite of you. She didn't like living in a small town.' As soon as she'd said it she knew she'd let out a can of worms. It could lead to all sorts of questions. But Elise made no comment, just smiled.

Claude was already fidgeting to be off. 'I have a lot to show Dani,' he told his mother when she protested that they had only just arrived.

'At least you must have a drink and maybe something to eat.'

'She has only just finished breakfast, this lazy girl,' he laughed.

Dani felt her colour rise but again Elise smiled indulgently.

'She works very hard, you tell me. So you must not rush her. Let her relax a little and enjoy her holiday.' She gave Claude a playful pat on his arm. 'He is such a slave driver, this boy. I don't know where he gets it from. Not from his father, I think.' This time her affectionate look was directed at Filipe. He nodded agreeably and continued to fill his pipe.

'Now we'll go to see my friend,' Claude said to Dani as they waved goodbye to his parents. 'He has many horses — you like horses, I think?'

'Great — but I'm not dressed for riding.'

'Why not?' he asked, opening the car door for her. 'You wear jeans and trainers. That is good.'

★   ★   ★

The stables and barns were run down but, as Gabin took them from one dilapidated building to another, he explained his vision of how he would restore them.

'It is the perfect countryside for riding. Here we will also have accommodation for guests. They will help with the horses, and in the evening they eat at my table.'

It sounded ambitious and Dani couldn't envisage it coming to fruition any time soon.

Gabin was undaunted. 'I own all you can see in every direction,' he said with pride.

They had no difficulty catching and harnessing a couple of horses and were soon galloping out into open countryside. Dani felt the wind in her hair and raced after Claude who was way ahead.

* * *

A couple of hours later they were sitting round the table in Gabin's stone floored kitchen with his wife, Sylvie, eating cheese with crusty bread, home-made fig jam from their own tree and bunches of Muscat grapes, all washed down with a plentiful supply of local wine. Dani was hungry after her ride and tucked into the feast. They laughed and chatted and Dani was as happy as she had ever been.

'Tomorrow we will visit my friend, Luc,' Claude announced when the meal was over. 'He owns a vineyard and makes some very special wine.'

'You have a lot of very interesting friends.' Dani laughed.

'And we will visit them all — if you do not mind, that is,' he said.

'Fine by me,' she said, feeling light-hearted at being with Claude and enjoying a different aspect of the countryside she knew only from visits with Lou and Nico.

It was almost dark when Claude drove home. He stopped the car just out of sight of the farmhouse and, leaning over, kissed Dani tenderly.

Looking into her eyes he said, 'This has been the most wonderful day. I am so much in love with you, Dani.'

'I love you too, Claude,' she told him.

8

It was Dani's first day back in the apartment. Francine had left early for an appointment but had insisted Dani should relax. Later they would talk through her plans to move to Paris.

It had been a wonderful few days with Claude, travelling around the countryside meeting his friends and experiencing new places. They were comfortable together and Dani felt their love had grown. There was no doubt in her mind now as to where her future lay.

While eating a late breakfast she received a text message from Alex. Staring at the screen, her heart clenched . . .

Your dad's not in school any more. Nobody seems to know why. The rumour's going round he's in trouble. Is it Zeta again? I know you've been worried about him.

She phoned Alex and as she waited for her to answer her hands started to shake and a great weight of guilt overwhelmed her.

She knew she shouldn't have left her dad. She should have realised something was wrong from his strange behaviour recently, not bringing work home from school, coming and going at different times. He'd been less stressed, happier.

But why? Meg had warned her. Yet she had been so wrapped up in her own concerns that she had disregarded all of it and taken the first opportunity to jump on a plane in her impatience to be back in Paris.

'I don't know any more than that,' Alex said. 'I was worried he might be ill, that's all. Shall I go round and see him? I like your dad. He was always kind to me at school even though I was one of the thick ones.'

'No, it's OK, Alex, I'll phone him. He hates a lot of fuss.'

Throughout the rest of the day Dani tried to contact him but got only his answerphone.

As soon as Francine came in that afternoon she rushed to meet her in the hallway.

'I have to go home, Mum!'

Francine stared at her. 'But you are only just back in Paris. I thought you were to stay at least another week?'

'There's something wrong with Dad.'

'What is wrong with him now?'

'I don't know — that's the problem.'

She showed her mum the text and Francine tried to phone Steve. Again there was no reply.

Dani could not contain her anxiety, wanting only to get back to England as quickly as possible and find out what was going on. She knew that her friend Alex wouldn't have alarmed her unnecessarily.

'Meg told me Dad was behaving strangely at school, too. He's been causing trouble in the science department, she said. You don't think he could have been suspended, do you?'

'I think it might be a possibility,' Francine said with genuine feeling. 'He cannot bear anyone to disagree with him.'

When Francine saw the look on Dani's face she quickly softened her manner.

'We must try Meg. She will know.'

Dani stopped her. 'No, Mum, I have to go home and find out for myself.'

Francine tried to reason with her, make her wait until they could get more information, but it was useless. Dani was already packing.

'Do you want me to come with you?' Francine asked, irritated and worried in equal measure.

'No, Mum, it wouldn't help.'

*   *   *

Three hours later she was sitting on the train coursing its way through the Channel Tunnel. She didn't have time to think about Claude. She hadn't even let him know she was on her way home.

Her mum would tell him.

Her dad was her priority now. She should never have left him. She should have known there was something amiss when he stopped bringing work home from school.

Now, sitting in the carriage, her head resting against the window, feeling the great weight of the water above her, she chided herself for not taking notice of her own instincts.

$$\star \quad \star \quad \star$$

Dani's dad met her at the station and was puzzled as to why she'd come home so suddenly before her holiday was over.

'What's going on, Dad?' Dani asked as soon as they got into the house.

He looked surprised. 'Nothing's going on. I don't know why you've come back.'

'I've been told you haven't been in school.'

He laughed. 'You shouldn't take notice of idle gossip, Dani.'

She persevered until finally he snapped

and told her to clear off back to Paris, slamming the door as he left the house!

He'd never spoken like that before and the shock brought tears to her eyes. It was now very clear that there was something seriously wrong.

Dani made herself a cup of tea and sat staring out over the garden, feeling very alone and trying to work out what to do.

Her mum was miles away. Claude wouldn't understand. Her dad seemed as if he had changed overnight from the lovable man she had always known into one she hardly recognised.

She felt she couldn't cope alone with this new situation. She needed to talk to someone.

★   ★   ★

Claude tried to phone Dani several times but she didn't pick up. She didn't want to discuss her dad's problems with anyone. If her mum couldn't understand her anxiety what chance had she of explaining it to Claude? He didn't know her dad. Nobody would understand how she felt.

Eventually she emailed Claude. That would allow her to say just what she wanted and no more. There would be no awkward questions to answer. His email back to her was puzzled. Why was she not answering her phone? She tried to stall him by saying her dad was ill and she'd had to come home to look after him. He was sympathetic but still couldn't understand why she wouldn't talk to him.

All night she lay in bed sleepless and worried. Steve hadn't come home until the early hours and she had no idea where he'd been. Eventually she fell into a restless sleep and when she woke he was gone again.

Next day he apologised for the way he'd spoken to her but still didn't open up. Dani didn't want to question him further for fear of arousing his anger again. Eventually she went to see Meg.

Meg hugged her and took her

through to her kitchen where they could talk.

'Meg, what's going on? Dad won't talk to me.'

'What have you heard?' Meg asked as she filled the kettle.

'Has he been off school?' Dani persisted.

Then she told Meg about the text and about the way her dad had behaved when she got home and that he was behaving oddly, not bringing school work home in the evenings — which was unheard of — and how he'd been going out every evening and not getting home until late.

Meg shook her head and sighed.

'These youngsters. They've nothing better to do than gossip!'

'No, Meg, Alex doesn't gossip. She's a good friend and she's concerned about Dad. She offered to go round and see him when I was in Paris but I stopped her.'

Meg gave Dani a questioning look. 'I thought you were staying in Paris for two weeks?'

'How could I stay after what Alex said?'

'Dani, sit down.' Meg pulled out a chair from the kitchen table.

Dani sank onto it. 'What?'

Meg sat opposite to her. 'Have you asked Alex what these rumours are, exactly?'

Dani shivered. 'Yes, but she said she didn't know any more than she'd already told me, that he's not in school after some trouble there. I think there was more and she was trying to protect my feelings, so I didn't push her. But you work at the school so I thought you'd know.'

Meg frowned.

'Is it really bad, Meg?' Dani asked tentatively.

'I'll be honest with you, Dani. Yes it is. Your dad hasn't been in school now for weeks. I don't actually know what's going on — he won't talk to me either — but we've been told that he's not coming back until after the summer holidays.'

'Why didn't you tell me before I went to Paris?'

Meg looked down and sighed. 'I should have done, but I wasn't sure then about any of it. We lab technicians don't get informed of such things, but I hear them talk. I hoped it would blow over by the time you got back, but I heard the other day that they've arranged for a supply teacher to take his classes.'

Dani put her hand to her mouth and gasped. 'Are you saying he's been suspended? Meg, what's he done?'

Meg looked reluctant then seemed to make a decision. She sat up straight.

'Dani, your dad's a good man . . . ' She hesitated. 'There was some trouble in the department, something to do with Zeta, and it seems your dad was the cause of it. He's not been himself for a long time now.'

Dani gripped her hands together to try to stop them shaking. 'Meg, you have to tell me.'

'I don't know, Dani. I've tried to talk

175

to him but all he says is that he's taking a break.'

'But that's not like Dad. He wouldn't do that!' she gasped.

'I know, and it worries me. I can't get through to him. There's something amiss but I don't know what it is. And I felt I'd already worried you enough. You have your own life to sort out.'

A shiver of fear went through Dani. This was why he'd been so keen on her going back to France. He hadn't been going into school at all and he didn't want her to know. But where had he been going?

Meg took Dani's hand across the table.

'Try not to worry too much. At least he seems better in himself. Whatever he's up to will all come out in the end.'

* * *

Francine was worried. It had been almost a week since Dani had rushed off home and, other than a phone call to say she'd arrived safely, Francine had not been able to speak to her daughter. Dani wasn't answering her phone and when she'd spoken to Steve he'd been evasive and unhelpful. Dani's emails had been guarded, never explaining what the trouble was that had sent her scurrying home.

Claude couldn't understand what was going on either. Dani had responded to his messages with love and affection, said how much she was missing him, but she never picked up or returned his calls. He knew there was something amiss and could only assume she was afraid that by talking to him she would be forced to explain things she preferred to keep to herself.

Also, he could not rid his mind of the thought that it might even have something to do with Ryan. She'd told him how upset Ryan had been when she'd ended their relationship. Maybe she was having second thoughts.

Eventually Francine decided she had to find out what was going on. If there was trouble and her daughter was having to deal with it, she needed to know. She would go to England.

Claude insisted on going with her. 'Unless you need me to stay here in your absence,' he said.

'I think it will all go along smoothly for a couple of days without us,' Francine told him. 'I would appreciate your company on this journey. I fear it may be unpleasant. And I think Dani would be pleased to see you — it may help her.'

Claude wasn't so sure about that, but he needed to find out first hand what was going on and whether Dani still felt for him as he did for her. And if Ryan was on the scene again then he needed to know.

* * *

Twenty-four hours later they stood in Steve's living room.

'You don't even know where she is?' Francine was gesticulating wildly, her accent becoming more pronounced the angrier she became.

Steve faced her across the room, his feet planted squarely on the carpet, determined not to be intimidated yet again by his volatile ex-wife.

'I've already told you, she's out. She *is* allowed to go out, isn't she?'

'But why has she not answered my calls?'

'Because she's sick of all the pressure you're putting on her. She came home for some peace.'

Francine flashed angry eyes.

'You are so pig-headed that you cannot see what is before you! Dani does not want this life here working at this bank. It is not right for her.'

'If you hadn't filled her head with all this fashion nonsense we wouldn't be having this argument! She'd be here, settling down to a proper career that will offer her a decent future.'

Francine dismissed his words with a toss of her head.

'And why did she have to come home in the middle of her holiday? What is all this trouble you are causing?'

'That is none of your business.'

Claude was pacing restlessly in the background. The last thing he wanted was to become embroiled in a family row. He wanted to see Dani.

Francine was about to launch into another attack when there was a knock at the door.

Steve opened it and Meg burst into the hall.

'Steve, you have to go to the hospital, quickly! Dani's there — no, no, she's not hurt. It's Ryan. His mother phoned Dani. He's been in an accident on his motorbike. They're both there now.'

She saw Francine standing behind him.

'Oh, Mrs Moore, I didn't know you were here. Will you go and talk to her? She's terribly upset.'

Steve seemed unable to keep pace with events and stared at Meg. It was Francine who took charge.

'We will go straight away. Claude, call a taxi.'

Francine turned to Meg who was about to pour out another long explanation about how Dani had been with her and they were having a cup of tea together when she got the call from Marianne.

'She shouldn't get involved. She's such a kind hearted girl. And she's been so worried about her father. And now this — '

Francine put up a hand to stop her.

'We must not waste time.'

Steve put an arm round Meg's shoulders and made her sit down. Francine gave him a sharp look. 'Are you coming or shall I go alone?'

'You'll be able to handle it better than me.'

'I'm coming with you,' Claude said. 'I must see Dani.'

* * *

Dani was in a waiting area sitting with a row of other people. When she saw Francine she stood up on unsteady legs and fell into her mum's arms.

'He's still unconscious. They won't let me see him,' Dani sobbed.

She was so upset she hadn't noticed Claude standing in the background. When Francine went to the machine to get Dani a cup of tea, he stood for a moment watching her, uncertain as to whether he should be there or if he was intruding.

Dani glanced towards the door where they'd taken Ryan. She moved slowly towards it wondering if she dare go in — then she saw Lisa walking purposefully towards her.

The two women stared at each other and Dani was shocked at how Lisa had changed. Her hair was frizzed and untidy. She looked older with dark circles under her eyes and her unmade up face was grey and drawn. She was even thinner now than when Dani had last seen her, her mouth an unpleasant hard line.

'What are you doing here?' she barked.

'To see how Ryan is,' Dani said feebly.

'Well, you needn't bother. He's with me now. Hasn't he told you?'

'Lisa, I don't think this is the place to fight. I came to see him as a friend, that's all.'

'Oh, yeah, and you expect me to believe that? He told me how cut up you were when he finished with you.'

'Lisa, please. Ryan's unconscious in there.'

'So long as you don't think you can grab him back again.'

Dani turned to go but Lisa hadn't finished. She grabbed her arm and twisted her back to face her. 'And don't go telling that father of yours any of our business. Do you hear me?'

Claude tensed, ready to step in if needed, but Dani twisted out of her grip, turned and walked back to where she'd been sitting, head bowed. Claude caught her in his arms and when she looked up and saw who it was she burst into tears. He held her until she'd calmed, wiped her tear-stained face, and took her hand.

'He is very important to you, your friend, Ryan?' he said gently.

She swallowed to try to control her voice.

'We've been friends for a long time,' she sobbed. Then seeing the look in his eyes she quickly added, 'I'm so glad you're here.' She paused, then in a small voice, added. 'I just want Ryan to be OK.'

Claude relaxed and hugged her close, whispering into her hair. 'Then we must help him all we can.'

Steve found Dani sitting beside Claude, and Francine talking to one of the nurses.

'I came to see Marianne,' he told Dani. 'Have you spoken to her?'

'I didn't know she was here,' Dani said.

'She's in the café. I found her wandering around the hospital looking for a coffee machine. She was in such a state I took her into the café to get her a drink. I'll go back and make sure she's all right. I just wanted you to know I'm here.'

Half an hour later Steve came back and sat beside Dani again.

'Ryan was in a police chase when he came off his bike — it was a stolen bike,' he told her, his expression full of concern. 'Dani, don't get involved. Let his mother deal with this.'

* * *

Francine and Claude booked into a hotel for the night. Next day when they arrived at the house Francine phoned the hospital in an attempt to stop Dani going back to visit again. When she put the phone down Dani jumped up.

'What is it, Mum? It's bad, isn't it?'

Francine put a steadying hand on Dani's shoulder and gave her a serious look.

'Yes, it is. But Ryan will recover. Now we have to talk about you.'

Dani let out a deep breath and felt

she couldn't make another decision to save her life. The shock of finding how much trouble Ryan was in and the mystery over what was happening to her dad had sapped all her strength. She slumped down heavily on the sofa.

Steve looked on, quietly anxious. Claude stood by, his face full of concern.

Francine took charge.

'Claude, please will you make some tea? We need something to sustain us.'

She sat beside Dani and took her hand.

Dani drank the tea Claude gave her without noticing what she was even doing. Her sadness seemed unbearable. She could hardly take it in. Ryan had told her how much she meant to him, had pleaded with her not to leave him. And she had pushed him away, not knowing how desolate he must have felt. And now he was lying in a hospital bed fighting for his life.

Claude and Francine tried to talk to Dani and persuade her that there was nothing more she could do for Ryan by staying. Lisa had made it clear that her visits were unwelcome, and he had a mother to care for him. But Dani stood firm.

'Dani, we must leave tomorrow. I have business to attend to,' Francine said, taking her hand.

'Mum, I keep telling you to go.'

'But why will you not come back with me? You tell me you want to work with me in Paris but yet you do nothing about it. You are still with your bank, I hear. What is it you want to do?'

Dani shook her head obstinately.

'I need to stay here, Mum. This is my home.'

At that moment Dani felt so drained she really didn't care where she lived or worked. She just wanted everyone to just leave her alone.

Francine sighed and turned to Claude.

'Can you not persuade her?'

Claude looked distraught.

'I have tried. She will not change her mind.'

Francine tried again. 'Dani, tell me

what is going on in your head. You were so set on joining me in Paris, and now you refuse to even consider it. I feel your father is putting pressure on you.'

Dani stared at Francine defiantly.

'Mum, I've made this decision all on my own and I've told you, I'm staying put.'

Francine shook her head in despair.

'Come, Claude, we must pack for tomorrow. If she does not want to come with us we must accept her decision and leave her alone.'

Dani breathed a sigh of relief — that was all she wanted.

Once they had left, Steve sat beside her.

'Dani, I think you should go to Paris and have this career in fashion if it's what you want.'

Dani shook her head and smiled. 'A few weeks ago you were all against it. What's changed?'

He shrugged. 'I've had time to think. I didn't want you giving up a good career on some whim. I know how persuasive your mother can be. But if it's really what you want, then go for it. All I want is for you to be happy.'

'Dad, I don't want to go to France.'

He gave her a questioning look.

'And this has nothing to do with me?'

She shook her head. 'Why should it be?'

'No reason at all. Everything's fine.'

He sat studying her.

'Dani, who is Claude? I gather he's somebody you met in France and become close to.'

She'd known this was going to crop up. She knew she ought to have explained it to her dad, but the time never seemed right and it only seemed to complicate matters.

'Dad, I'm sorry. I should have told you about him. But really it doesn't matter now.'

'I think it does. He seemed a decent man who genuinely cares about you. Dani, are you sure you're not making a big mistake staying here?'

'Claude and I got on well together

and it might have developed into something more — but it's over.'

'It needn't be.'

'I'm not going to France to live. I probably won't ever see him again.

'Dani, don't make any rash decisions. You were keen to go to Paris before all this business with Ryan. Why have you changed your mind so suddenly?'

'I haven't, Dad. There are too many things to keep me here.' She gave him a questioning look. 'Does this have something to do with Claude? Do you think packing me off to France will distance me from Ryan? Is that what this is all about?'

He gave a wry smile.

'Claude would certainly be a better bet for a son-in-law than Ryan.'

She couldn't help laughing.

'You're always trying to run my life for me. I'm a big girl now and I can look after myself.'

He became more serious. 'Yes, you are but I'll always be your dad and I can't stop protecting you and wanting the best for you. But I suppose you must do as you think fit.'

'I want to forget all about Claude and not talk about him any more. I want to stay here and let everything carry on as normal.'

He gave her a sceptical look but when she glared at him he changed it to a forced smile.

'OK, message understood. Just so long as you're doing what you want to do and not making any of your decisions on my account. If you really don't want to change direction then I'm more than happy with that.'

Her face creased into a smile. He seemed so upbeat and happy that Dani didn't want to spoil the moment. When he was ready, he would tell her what was going on.

In the meantime she could continue with her life as normal and settle down again. It had all been a silly pipe dream, and she wondered how she could have had her head turned so easily.

'Shall we have another takeaway

tonight? I really don't feel like cooking,' she said, smiling.

'You mean I get to eat some proper food, not this healthy stuff you keep telling me is good for me?' Steve retorted.

Then they were laughing and it felt almost as if the last few months had never happened.

★　★　★

Steve had just left the house when Francine and Claude appeared next day to say goodbye, bags packed and ready to leave. Claude looked so downcast Dani felt her resolve weaken. She managed to give him a hug and then looked into his eyes, those eyes she loved and had hoped one day to see every day of her life. Now all that had changed. He was going out of her life, and she was staying here.

He took hold of her hands, his expression tortured and regretful.

'Please change your mind, Dani. I

want us to be together. Is it not what you want too? It was what you wanted once. Do you not love me any more?' His voice was so quiet, yet somehow that made his words all the more powerful.

Danis own voice dropped to a whisper.

'Claude, I don't know what I feel. Everything's changed. I'm sorry, but I can't make any commitments at the moment. I can't explain.' A lump was forming in her throat preventing her from saying anything else.

He hugged her close. 'You must take all the time you need, my darling. When you feel ready let me know and I will come for you. I will wait.'

'No, Claude, you must go home and forget about me!'

Tears were threatening but she knew she had to be strong. He was a good man and she hated what she was doing to him, but to give him false hopes would have been wrong.

Claude dropped her hands and stood

away from her, his expression now one of resignation, his voice steady.

'I see that you no longer want us to be together. I think maybe you have not quite made up your mind about many things. This gives me great pain but I respect your wishes.'

A cold chill made her skin prickle. She knew what he was referring to. He thought she still had feelings for Ryan, but she didn't have the energy to dispute it.

Francine was getting anxious.

'We must leave now, my dear. We will miss our train if we do not.' Francine hugged Dani again and looked closely at her tear-stained face and shook her head. 'Take care, and remember I am always there to listen.'

Dani hugged her close. The warmth and smell of her mum was comforting. She wished so much she was staying, and that her mum and dad were together and could sort all this trouble out. But it wasn't to be, so she let her go and watched as they loaded their bags into the waiting taxi.

Dani closed the door and climbed the stairs. Her bed was still unmade but it didn't matter. She threw herself onto the crumpled quilt and burst into tears — confused, helpless and her mind in turmoil — but above all feeling unbearable sadness.

★ ★ ★

Dani had only just managed to control her anguish when the doorbell rang.

Alex stood apprehensively on the step. Dani pulled her in and hugged her.

'I didn't know whether you wanted to see me or not . . . ' Alex said hesitantly.

'Of course I do,' Dani said.

'Well, you didn't when I phoned yesterday.'

Dani looked down.

'No, sorry about that. I was having a bad day.'

'You don't look much better today.'

Dani tried to smile as she took Alex

into the back room where they collapsed into the big comfy chairs.

'Has your mum gone yet?'

'Yes, a couple of hours ago.'

'Are they getting on any better? Your mum and dad, I mean.'

Dani shrugged. 'I don't know. They didn't fight as much. They both seemed more concerned about me than about each other.'

Alex frowned. 'Are you really going to stay here? I can't believe you're giving up the chance to live in Paris.'

'I know, Alex, but with everything that's happened it's changed the way I see things.'

'What, you mean your dad?'

Dani frowned. 'What was that text about, Alex? What exactly is everyone talking about?'

'Look, Dani, I've told you I don't want to get into all this. It's what made us fall out yesterday.'

Dani felt anger rising. She jumped up and stood over Alex. 'You brought me back here with your text, and now you don't want to talk about it?'

Alex was on the defensive.

'Dani, stop shouting at me and sit down. Look, I've only heard the rumours and you know what they're like. I thought as a friend I ought to warn you about what was going on at home while you were away. I didn't know you were going to jump on the next train and come home!'

Dani became angry. 'I did that because you made it sound really bad. But you still haven't told me what they're saying.'

Alex got up and backed away. 'Look, it's mainly Lisa and you know what she's like.'

Alex was trying to pacify her now. Dani could detect that she regretted starting the scare that had brought her home.

'Yes, I know what Lisa's like,' Dani said crossly. 'But what about Dad? What are they saying about him?'

'I have to go,' Alex announced. Shrugging into her jacket she went towards the door. 'Why don't you ask him? Then at least you'll get the truth.'

Dani followed her. 'I will, but I still want to know what they're saying about him.'

Alex turned. 'OK, but don't blame me if you don't like it! He's supposed to have lost his temper at school with Zeta and there was a big scene then he stormed out. Some of the kids saw it happen. And he hasn't been in school since.'

Dani could feel the colour draining from her face. She felt light-headed and sank back into the chair.

'Do you think he's been suspended, Alex?'

'Well, they say there's no smoke without fire.'

Dani closed her eyes.

'Look, Dani, you asked me for my opinion. I said you wouldn't like it.'

'Alex, I think you ought to go.'

'I'm going. I can't make you out these days. There's no talking to you. You've changed.'

'Yes, I have. I'm sorry, Alex, but I need to be on my own.'

She got up and opened the door and Alex strutted out in a huff.

9

By the time Steve came home that evening Dani had worked herself into a state. She had to confront him, make him tell her. She could not live with rumours any longer.

If what Alex was telling her was true, then she needed to know. And if he wasn't going to school where was he spending all his time? There had to be an explanation, and only he could supply it. Once she knew what they were up against she'd be able to handle it.

Having made up her mind she felt stronger — but when he came into the kitchen, her hands were still clammy and her stomach churning.

He poured himself a beer from the fridge and plonked himself down at the kitchen table. Dani stood, uncertain, by the sink pretending to clear the dishes that had been dumped there.

'Dad, I want to know what's going on.'

'What's going on where?'

'Dad, you know what I mean. What's really going on with school?'

'I don't know. Nothing much, I suspect as it's almost the end of term. If you've changed your mind and decided after all that you do want to go to France and join your mother, I'd be delighted. I've found out all about it. I'm satisfied you'll get decent training and a good future. That's all I've ever wanted for you, to be happy and successful.'

She felt anger rising.

'Dad, don't keep putting me off. You have to tell me why you've been out of school for weeks.'

His expression changed. He held her gaze but seemed lost for words. Finally he straightened and took a deep breath. 'Dani, there is nothing for you to worry about except your own future.'

'Dad, stop it! Will you please just tell

me? I'm not a child any more. I've heard the gossip. Since before I went to Paris you were going out in the morning and coming back in the afternoon but you weren't going to school. Why are you lying?'

'Who told you that?'

'Everyone is telling me! Everyone seems to know what's going on except me!'

He sighed. 'Dani, I'm trying not to worry you. You have enough on your mind without me.' There was a long pause as they looked at each other and a cold hand of fear clutched at her heart.

Eventually he spoke. 'OK. I can see you won't let this rest, so here goes. I had a bust-up with Zeta. It wasn't the first. I knew it was my fault. Somehow I haven't been myself recently. I stormed out of school and next day I simply couldn't face going in again. The head persuaded me to see my doctor who told me I had to take time out of school, said I was suffering from stress, so I'm on sick leave until they sort me out.'

Dani let out a long breath. Her dad hadn't been suspended. He wasn't in trouble. He hadn't done anything wrong. Her relief was overwhelming!

Yes, he was ill. He needed care to get him well again, but she could provide that. She would give him all the care she could and soon have him back to his normal self.

'So what happens now?' she asked him.

'At best I'll get better and they'll have me back. Or it might be goodbye to teaching.'

'But, Dad, what would you do if that happens?'

'I'll have to find something else,' he said.

'But you've always been so dedicated to teaching. What else could you do?'

'Oh, I have some ideas.' He was becoming more animated. 'You want to know what I've been doing these last few weeks when you thought I was going to school? Well, I've been going to the library. I've always wanted to compile a book on rare insects and never had time. Now I do have time. Then I go for walks on the heath and through the woods.'

'Well, you won't have to keep up that pretence any more. You can write your book at home. And I'll be here to take care of you.'

Dani could feel her throat constricting. Teaching was his life. He was a good teacher, a caring teacher. How could some stupid woman bring all that to an end? How glad she was that she had stayed. He needed her now more than ever and she would not desert him.

Dani went to him and hugged him.

'They don't deserve to have you as a teacher. You're the best and they should appreciate you.'

He looked at her seriously. 'Is this why you've decided to stay? You want to keep an eye on me? Dani, you mustn't do this. If they decide to get rid of me

I'll find something else to do. You go off and pursue your career. I want you to be successful and make me proud of you.'

She looked down into those concerned eyes. Why had she ever resented his protection and ambition for her? She was very lucky to have him as her dad.

'No, I don't want to do it any more. I want to stay here and get back to normal. You were right. I have a good job and I'll stick with it. Back to work on Wednesday and no looking back.'

She was glad now that she'd added the extra days onto her two weeks. It gave her that little bit of time to relax now that all the trauma was over.

He took her hand. 'Whatever you want to do is fine by me. Just so long as you're doing it for yourself. You must promise me you'll not base your decisions on me. Promise me.'

'Dad, I'll do what I want to do. You should know that by now.'

He shook his head and smiled. 'Yes,

you're a very determined woman, just like your mother.'

★   ★   ★

Next day Dani summoned up the courage to phone Alex and ask her to come round.

'I'm sorry about yesterday, honestly I am.'

'Dani, I'm sorry, too. I didn't mean to be so nasty. It's just I don't know what to say to you any more. I'm sorry if I alarmed you with that text, but it was all true.'

She promised to come around after work, around six o'clock. Dani cheered up.

'And I promise I won't be grumpy. I want to know what everybody's up to. I really do need to get back into things.'

'When do you start work again?'

'I'm back on Wednesday. I've decided to stay put. And just so you know, Dad is on sick leave. He hasn't done anything wrong. So you can ignore

anything else you've heard. See you at
six.'

⋆   ⋆   ⋆

Dani and Alex were sitting in the back
room with the French windows open,
enjoying a lovely summer evening.

'Right, I want to talk about you.
We've had enough about my worries
and moods. Tell me about Morley's. I
always feel it would be a happy place to
work. Much more fun than in a bank,'
Dani said.

Alex pulled a face. 'It's OK. They
don't pay much and the supervisor's a
bit grumpy, but we have a laugh. All the
staff are ancient, as you know. I mean,
really old. You wouldn't believe what
some of them talk about in their tea
break. Really boring stuff like what they
had for dinner last night and the price
of shampoo at Wilko's. God, Dani, I
hope we never get like that! Do you
think we will?'

Dani burst out laughing. It was good

to talk nonsense with Alex again.

'I envy you, Alex. Settled in your own home with Adam. Not like me, always changing my mind.'

'What do you really want, Dani? I know you said not to talk about you, but we have to. Do you really want to go on working at that bank? You seemed so keen on going to France. And what about Claude? You haven't given up on him too, have you?'

Dani went quiet.

'Can we not talk about Claude, please, Alex?'

'OK, but what about the rest of it, the new job and everything?'

'I can't leave Dad at the moment.'

'I thought he was OK about you going now.'

'Yes, but I think he's just putting up a brave front because he wants me to do what makes me happy. He doesn't want me to put my life on hold for him.'

'Wouldn't you rather be in France with your mum, though?'

'No, it all seems like a strange dream

now. I can't believe I was actually contemplating it.'

'It's Ryan, too, isn't it?'

'I don't know. We've been friends for a long time. But he's with Lisa now. I just can't stop feeling it was because of me he had the accident.'

'How do you make that out?'

'He was really cut up when I finished with him. He pleaded with me to give it another go.'

'Look, Dani, don't keep torturing yourself. OK, your dad's been stressed, but he's better now he's out of that school. And Ryan's stupid but he's out of the coma and he'll recover. It can't all be your fault. Get on with your life and let them sort out theirs. I wish my mum did what yours does. I'd be there like a shot — go for it, Dan!'

'No, Dad was right. I'd be silly to give up a good career on a whim. How could I get excited about a fashion show when Dad's at home all on his own? At least by carrying on here I'll be looking after him like he's always looked after me.'

'Are you still going to look for something else? You said you didn't enjoy working in the bank.'

'I don't know. I'll stay put for a while. I just want a settled life until I know Dad's all right. Then I might look around.'

Alex sighed. 'Well, I'm here for you, Dani. We'll always be friends, you and me.'

★   ★   ★

Dani was feeling positive about going back to work the next day. She wanted to get her life back on track after all the trauma of the past weeks. But today she was going shopping with Alex. Dressed in jeans and a crop top, as the weather was warm, she made her way to the bus stop.

Alex was waiting, and seeing her smiling face made Dani feel better.

'How are you feeling about tomorrow?' Alex asked when they were seated on the bus.

'Now I've made my mind up I'm looking forward to settling down again.'

'You sound happy again,' Alex said.

'I am but I'm a bit worried about the gossip.'

'What gossip?'

'You know . . . about my dad.'

'How are they going to know about that? Your bank's in Chelmsford, miles away. Why are you so worried?'

'Well, you said it was all over the internet. I feel as if the whole world knows about my dad losing his rag in front of the entire school and then not going in again,' she confessed. 'And Ryan's accident was in the papers, too.'

'Oh, come on, Dani, You can't be responsible for other people messing up.'

'But it's not *other people*, is it? It's my dad and my ex-boyfriend. Somebody's bound to know and they'll give me pitying looks and avoid me.'

'It was weeks ago. It'll all be forgotten now.'

They got off the bus in the Square

and began to walk towards the High Street.

Alex shook her head. 'I don't know why you didn't go to Paris. I know you want to look after your dad, but you said yourself that he's never at home these days.'

Dani was thoughtful. 'I hardly see him at all. He's completely absorbed in this book he's writing and he prefers the library. But what I can't understand is where he goes in the evenings. He's hardly ever in then either.'

'Maybe he's got a girlfriend — have you thought about that?'

Dani stared at her friend.

'That would explain the phone calls, too.'

'What phone calls?'

'He spends a lot of time on the phone late at night, and when he thinks I can hear he talks really quietly or hangs up and looks sort of guilty. And I often pick up the house phone when it rings and then it goes dead.'

'Couldn't you check the number?'

'I did and it said the number was withheld.'

'I reckon it's a lady friend.'

Dani felt uneasy. She'd never considered her dad could have another woman in his life. It changed everything.

'Can we go and have a coffee?' She was surprised to hear the quiver in her own voice.

Alex frowned. 'Look, I might be wrong. Why don't you ask him?'

'I couldn't do that, Alex. It would be too embarrassing. What if he didn't have one? What if we were completely wrong?'

'Look, it's not the end of the world if he has. He's bound to meet someone one day. He's not going to live on his own for ever.'

However hard Dani tried, she couldn't stop her mouth from quivering. She felt exposed standing in the middle of the high street, as if everyone could see her anguish.

Alex took her arm and steered her into a café. Dani sat at a table while Alex went to order food. She kept her head down, hoping nobody would recognise her, and wished she was at home and could have a good bawl in private.

★   ★   ★

Next morning Dani was surprised at how good it felt to be going back to work. She made her way up in the lift to the sixth floor of the bank and settled at her desk. One by one her colleagues came over and asked how her holiday had been. By lunchtime she felt she had hardly been away and that the past two weeks were something she had only dreamed.

She met Molly as usual for lunch. Molly was in a different department, but the two girls had joined the bank on the same day and quickly became friends.

'Hi, Dani, how was your holiday?' Molly said as soon as she saw her.

'Fine.' Now she was back to reality she didn't want to dwell on the past.

They collected their food from the

self-service counter and found a table in the busy canteen.

'OK, so fill me in on what's changed here since I've been away,' Dani said, determined not to let the conversation centre on her.

'Does anything ever change here?'

'Well, I've got some news for you,' Dani said with a smirk on her face.

'You have?'

'I've been offered a promotion. Mr Miller's just spoken to me in his office.'

Molly looked surprised. 'But you were dead set on leaving a few weeks ago. You said you wanted a change of career.'

Molly was the only person at work Dani had mentioned this to. She was a good and trusted friend and Dani had needed someone to confide in — but she hadn't told her anything about Claude or the possibility that she might move to Paris. Now there was no need to tell her any of it.

'I confess I was feeling a bit restless,' Dani said. 'But I'm really tempted by this new offer. It'll mean I'll be working with the public, not stuck in an office all day.'

'Well, I'm really pleased for you, Dani, if it's what you really want, and I'm ever so glad you're not leaving. Who would I have to gossip with at lunchtime if you left?'

Molly beamed and Dani felt a warmth spreading through her. It was good to feel settled again.

★　★　★

When Dani got home Steve was sorting the mail at the dining room table and looked up at her as she entered the room.

'You look pleased with yourself.'

She grinned. 'I am.'

'Go on, then, tell me.'

'Well, I had a nice lunch with Molly today — and guess what?'

'I have no idea,' he said, shaking his head with amusement. 'You'll have to tell me.'

'I've been promoted! And it means I

get to work with customers, at last.'

His smile broadened.

'That's great news. So now you can settle down again and stop searching for that elusive something else.'

'That's what I intend to do.'

After telling him a bit more about her earlier interview and what the job entailed she hauled two big files out of her bag and went up to her bedroom to study them.

Her phone rang and it was Alex.

'How's it going, Dani?'

'Good,' Dani told her friend. 'And guess what? I've been offered a promotion!'

'Hey, it sounds like you made the right decision in the end then,' Alex said. 'Want to come over for a gossip? It seems you've lots to tell me.'

'I'd love to but they've given me loads of stuff to read. It's going to take all evening.'

'Wow, you do sound keen!' There was a long pause. 'Have you heard from Claude?'

Dani tensed. 'Alex, I told you, Claude and I are done. We'll never be together. I told him I'm not going to live in Paris and he's obviously taken me at my word. Can we leave it at that? I have to go, Alex. Maybe see you Saturday?'

Dani didn't feel quite so upbeat as she pulled one of the files out of her bag and began to thumb through it. As she struggled to concentrate, thoughts of Paris and Claude and what might have been kept intruding.

Thinking of Claude almost broke her heart and she felt the tears pricking.

10

Ryan was out of hospital and making a good recovery. Dani hadn't seen him since he'd been discharged several weeks ago, but he was getting better and that was all that mattered.

She flung her bag down in the hall. It had been a tiring day trying to get the hang of this new job she'd been promoted to. It was more challenging and she enjoyed the contact she had with the public — but still she felt restless.

She hung her jacket at the end of the stairs and picked up the letters from the floor. Her dad wasn't in again. She was beginning to wonder if her being here made any difference to him at all as they hardly ever saw each other. Yet he did seem more relaxed and cheerful. He was obviously getting well and would probably be fit to start school again soon. Perhaps it would be better if he didn't go back to teaching and carried on writing books. She'd never seen him as content as he'd been these last few weeks.

There were no letters from her mum, but she'd spoken to her last night. She tried not to even think about there being anything from Claude. She really had to get a grip! She had told him their relationship was over, after all, so why on earth would he keep pursuing her?

The local paper was still wedged in the letterbox. She tugged at it, trying to release it without tearing it. Finally she freed it and glanced at the front page. Her heart stopped.

A large picture of Ryan stared out at her, his look challenging as always.

She read the headline above it. He'd been convicted of possessing stolen property. The police had found three motorbikes in a shed behind Lisa's flat. Ryan was going to prison!

Her mind was in turmoil. How would

he survive that? He'd be mixing with all sorts of criminals and would get himself into even more trouble. She could see no future for him now.

Was that her fault, too? If she hadn't ended their relationship, he wouldn't be with Lisa. If she hadn't hurt him, he would still be working with Brad, fixing motorbikes and leading a normal life.

Oh, where was her dad when she needed him? She paced the room. Why had Ryan got himself into this mess when he had a good job and the prospect of a decent life? His mum would be beside herself!

Eventually she could contain herself no longer. She had to find her dad. She needed his reassuring presence. She grabbed her key and, slamming the door behind her, raced along the road towards the library.

He wasn't there.

Next thing she was hammering on Marianne's door and praying she'd be in. If she couldn't find her dad, she'd talk to Ryan's mum. She'd be in a state too, and they could console each other.

Dani stared in shock when it was her dad Steve opened the door!

'What are you doing here?' He stood aside to let her in. 'How did you know I was here?'

'I didn't,' she murmured.

They stood facing each other in the small square of hallway, both at a loss for words.

'You've seen the paper?' he said at last.

'Yes, I couldn't find you. So I came to see Marianne, to see if I can help.'

'She's very upset. And you are, too, I can see.'

He put an arm round her shoulders and led her into the living room.

Marianne was sitting in a chair looking red-eyed and pale. She looked up when they entered the room, a hint of a smile lightening her distress.

'Oh, Dani, I'm glad you came,' she said, standing up. 'You were fond of him too, I know.'

Steve hovered in the background as

they hugged each other and Dani felt some comfort in their shared pain.

'It's so awful, seeing him like that in the paper,' Marianne said, still holding Dani's hands, her mouth beginning to quiver. 'After all that's happened, just when he's recovering from his accident and beginning to look well again.'

Dani couldn't think of anything to say. There were no words of comfort that seemed appropriate and her mind was still numb with shock.

'Your dad's been so kind,' Marianne continued, struggling to hold back the tears. 'I don't know what I would have done without him these past few months.'

In a flash Dani's mind cleared. That was it! This was where her dad came in the evenings. Alex's words echoed in her head as she stared at the distraught woman. Her dad and Marianne? Was she pleased, relieved, embarrassed? She seemed to be experiencing all at the same time, her confusion overwhelming her. How could she have been so naïve?

She stood there, unable to move, not knowing how to react. Directing her eyes to the floor she slowly released herself from Marianne's grip.

'Why don't you take Dani home?' Marianne said softly, looking towards Steve. 'She's had a nasty shock, too. Take her home and look after her. She needs you.'

Steve put an arm round Dani's shoulder.

'Come on, love. Let's go home.'

She let him lead her out of the house and they walked home in silence. He made tea and sat quietly with her at the kitchen table while she drank it. She couldn't bring herself to look at him. They were both at a loss how to continue.

Finally Steve spoke. 'Marianne's suffered over the past weeks of the trial. She's a good person and she has tried with Ryan, Dani. She doesn't deserve this.'

'Nobody deserves this,' Dani agreed.

'Nice little business he had going.' Steve didn't say Ryan deserved what was coming to him or that he'd warned her against him, but she knew that was what he was thinking.

'Dad, he's going to prison. How will Marianne cope with that?'

'He won't. He's been given a suspended sentence. I've had a word with Brad and he's going to consider giving Ryan another chance. And Ryan wants that. I'm doing everything I can for his mother's sake.'

'Dad, have you been spending a lot of time there? Is that where you go in the evenings? Why didn't you tell me? Why all the secrecy?'

He covered her hand with his across the table.

'I didn't want to upset you, Dani.'

She shook her head slowly. 'You're always trying to protect me, Dad. But I prefer the truth.'

He hung his head. 'Yes, I know. I'm sorry.'

She gave a watery smile. 'Marianne needs someone to support her, and I'm glad it's you.'

His expression changed to a mixture of surprise and relief. Then he got up and was fishing in the bin for something. Eventually he brought out the newspaper she had deposited in there earlier. She got up to try to stop him but he was determined.

'Look, I have something I want to show you, something that may cheer you up a little.' He laid the paper on the kitchen table in front of them and thumbed through it until he found what he was looking for, then pointed out a small column half way down the page.

It had the heading, *Local author publishes book on rare insects.*

She read it and, as the words sank in, a smile began to form on her lips and a warm glow spread through her. She turned to him with tears in her eyes. 'Dad, you've got your book published. That's wonderful!'

Then she read it again just to be sure. 'Why didn't you say? When did you find out?'

'Yesterday. But I didn't think it was

the right time to broadcast it with this other news. I knew you'd be upset, and Marianne as well. It didn't seem right that I should be getting such good news when you both had to cope with this.'

'So, when are you going back to school?'

'I'm not. I've finished with teaching.'

'Dad, you can't do that. They have to let you back now that you're better.'

'I'm not going back into teaching because I don't want to. It's my decision.'

She stared in disbelief. 'What will you do?'

He stood facing her, a smirk on his face.

'Well, the publisher is going to take my second book on local history and has commissioned me to write two more. What do you think of that? Your old dad isn't finished yet.'

He had such an air of satisfaction she felt a surge of love and pride. 'Dad, that's great.'

'Yes, but that isn't all.'

'What, there's more?' she mocked. 'Tell me.'

'One of the librarians is going on maternity leave and Janet, the other one, will need help so they've asked me if I can take over her job. I've agreed and I start next Monday. So now you have it all.'

No, I don't have it all, Dani thought. *He's missing out a big chunk here but it will do for now.*

He was well again and happy and had a future and she'd get used to the Marianne thing eventually. If she was to have the life she wanted, she couldn't begrudge it to her dad.

A feeling of elation swept through her as she suddenly realised what this meant. She was free to do as she pleased. Her dad no longer needed her. It had been fairly obvious for some time and now she knew why. He had Marianne.

All her ambition for progressing within the bank suddenly evaporated. She no longer had to talk herself into a career that was wrong for her.

He must have read her thoughts.

'And now we have to talk about you and your future, Dani. I know you're not happy and I know where you really want to be. I understand why you changed your mind about France. You were worried about me, and I appreciated that. I like having you here, but above all I want you to be happy. I really think you should go off and try your luck with this fashion thing.

'You can always come back if it doesn't work out. But if you don't try it you will never know.'

'But do you still think it would be a bad move?'

'No. At first I did but now I can see it's the best thing. You're a sensible young woman, Dani. You know what you want. I have to respect that. I don't want you resenting me for stopping you from having the life you feel is right for you.'

'I wouldn't do that, Dad. But will you be all right on your own here?' She still wasn't convinced.

'Of course I will. I'm fit and well now. Teaching was very demanding and I'm ready for a change.'

And you have Marianne, she thought but found she was no longer unhappy about the idea.

'So, you see I'll be fine. And Paris isn't that far away. I can come and see you and you always know where I am if you need me.'

'Dad — I really do want to go.'

'So you should go, no more arguments. Start packing and I'll book your flight.'

'You won't get rid of me that quickly, Dad — I have to work my notice,' Dani said, hugging him.

★   ★   ★

The weeks before Dani could leave the bank and begin her new life in France were a mixture of excitement and regrets.

Mr Miller was horrified. He told her how well she'd done so far and how she could progress right to the top if she continued with them.

Molly tried not to show how much she would miss her but couldn't hide the way she felt. Alex said she had done the right thing and told her she was pleased for her — then burst into tears!

One person she was not expecting to see was Zeta. Dani was in the house alone. Steve had gone to the library for his first morning on duty. Dani had just got out of the shower when the bell rang. Struggling into her towelling wrap she ran down the stairs to open the door. Zeta stood on the doorstep, tall and elegant as always, with that familiar haughty tilt of her head.

'Hello, Dani, is your father at home?'

'No, he's at the library,' Dani said, wondering what sort of trouble this was going to bring up.

Zeta gave a tentative smile but continued to stand there. Good manners forced Dani to ask her in, although she couldn't think what Zeta would want with her. Zeta stepped into the hallway and then followed Dani into the back room where she stood a moment in hesitation.

'Is there anything I can help you with?' Dani said automatically. Whatever Zeta wanted with her dad was none of her business and she really didn't want to get involved.

Zeta pulled herself up to her full height and pursed her lips in a manner Dani was familiar with from school days.

'I wanted to talk to him,' she said, in her superior tone of voice.

'Zeta, he's finished with school, given his notice. He won't be bothering you again.'

Dani could hardly believe she was talking to her former teacher this way! The woman was beginning to look uncomfortable, at a loss how to proceed. She obviously hadn't expected to be spoken to like that by a former pupil.

'Dani, I haven't come to cause trouble,' she said in a more conciliatory tone. 'I came to tell him how sorry I am that things went as they did.'

'Well, it's a bit late now,' Dani said, surprising herself again with her boldness.

Zeta continued, ignoring Dani's comment. 'I feel in some way responsible. We had our differences and I should have listened to him.'

'Yes, you should.' Dani was becoming more emboldened by this woman's attitude and angry that she should be so patronising when she had caused her dad so much distress.

'It was his obstinate manner I found difficult. He wouldn't co-operate.' Again it seemed that Zeta was trying to justify her behaviour.

'He was ill,' Dani said. 'That's why he hasn't been in school. He was suffering from stress.'

Zeta nodded furiously. 'I know that now, and I should have made allowances.'

'He loved teaching,' Dani said. 'And now he won't go back.'

'That's what I came for. I wanted to

try to persuade him to change his mind. He was a good teacher. He had a great deal of experience.' Zeta paused. Then with a quieter sincerity Zeta said, 'He should have been promoted to head of department, not me.'

Dani felt a sudden sympathy for this woman who she had considered was responsible for all her dad's problems.

Zeta continued, her voice having lost all its aggression. 'He brought a lot of common sense into the department and did influence some of my decisions. He will be a great loss to the school.'

Dani sighed. 'It's too late now. He's made his decision, and he seems happy with it.'

'Dani, will you tell him we miss him?'

'Yes, of course I will. I think he'll be pleased you thought highly of him.'

'Thank you.' Zeta slowly turned to leave.

Dani stopped her. 'Why don't you come back another day and tell him yourself? He would appreciate that.'

Dani saw her out and wandered back

up the stairs. It pleased her to hear what she had always known — that her dad was a good teacher and well respected.

★ ★ ★

Dani said a tearful goodbye to Meg with the promise of coming back often to see her.

Alex was overjoyed when Dani insisted she come and visit once she was settled.

'Mum has a big apartment and I want to show you everything,' Dani told her.

'I'm so envious,' Alex admitted. 'You must send me long emails about your new life.'

There was just one more person Dani had to see before she left for Paris next day.

Marianne was hanging out washing in her tiny back yard and was delighted when Dani appeared. They sat on a couple of canvas chairs outside her back door and Dani was pleased to see how much better Marianne looked than the last time she'd seen her.

'Your dad's been so kind,' she said. 'I don't think I could have got through these last months without him.'

'I think you've helped Dad, too,' Dani said.

Marianne looked questioningly at Dani. 'You don't mind, do you, Dani?'

Dani smiled. 'Of course not. Why would I when it makes Dad so much happier?'

'I'm glad he's decided to give up teaching,' Marianne continued. 'It was getting him down. He's more relaxed now he's made that decision.'

'How's Ryan doing?' Dani asked.

Marianne smiled. 'Lisa's expecting a baby. Did you know? I'm going to be a granny.' She was quick to reassure Dani. 'Ryan's determined to be a good dad, not like his own dad. And Lisa's changed. It might be the making of both of them.'

'I hope so,' Dani said.

Marianne shook her head and sighed.

'Lisa's not such a bad girl, you know. I feel sorry for her in a way. She's not had much of a life. I think once she's got a family of her own she'll act more responsibly. And she says she'll stand by Ryan if he does goes to prison.'

'But that may not happen,' Dani said.

'Not if your dad has anything to do with it.'

Dani told Marianne of her plans before they got up and hugged each other goodbye.

'Look after Dad, won't you?' Dani said, suddenly feeling tearful.

Marianne pulled away and gave her an affectionate smile.

'You don't have to ask that, Dani. Of course I will. We're very fond of each other, you know.'

'I think it's more than that?' Dani said, giving her a knowing look.

'Yes, you could be right.' Marianne blushed. 'So now you must go off and live your own life. There's no need for you to worry about your dad any more.'

Dani left feeling both happy and sad

at the same time. Everyone seemed to be sorting their lives out.

All she had to do now was sort her own.

11

Dani's emotions were in turmoil. Here she was at the airport waiting for a flight to take her to a new life. She'd been so absorbed in packing and sorting everything out over the past few weeks she'd hardly had time to think about it.

Francine had been delighted when Dani had told her she was on her way. Alex had kept her on a high with all her talk about fashion and Paris and all the glamour, but would the day-to-day life she was about to embark on be anything like that? She doubted it.

She'd lost Claude. He had obviously taken her at her word and forgotten all about her. She couldn't blame him after the way she'd treated him, constantly changing her mind.

Francine hadn't mentioned Claude at all and Dani suspected there was a reason for this. He would be involved with some other woman. Francine had warned her on that very first day when she'd met him, told her he loved all the ladies and that she didn't want her to get hurt. Dani hadn't spoken about him with her mum recently. Until she knew for certain that he had moved on she clung to the hope he might still be waiting for her. Yet she knew it was a vain hope.

She browsed the bookshop and bought a paperback to read on the plane. She checked and re-checked her ticket. When they called her flight she made her way to the boarding gate.

Soon enough she would have all the answers.

Finally she was in her seat, hand luggage stowed overhead, peering out of the tiny window as they taxied towards the runway. The whirring of the plane's engine calmed her, the force of take-off pushing her back in her seat. Her stomach lurched until the plane steadied.

'Good afternoon, passengers, this is your captain speaking — '

Dani wasn't interested in what he had to say. The weather could do what it liked. She'd get there when she got there. She had too much on her mind. But he carried on and then repeated it all in French, a language that from now on she would have to adopt as her own. There was no turning back this time. This was it.

The hostess placed a hot pasty in front of her. She'd ordered it out of habit. Slowly she peeled open the packet and picked at the tasteless offering in the hope it would settle the churning in her stomach. She wouldn't be able to chat to Alex every day now. Dad wouldn't be there in the background keeping her feet firmly on the ground. The food stuck in her throat and she had to swallow hard to get it down.

It was supposed to be a new beginning, what she had desperately wanted, but it felt more like the end.

The end of Dad's protection, of old friends and home and everything she'd known.

★ ★ ★

She switched her phone back on as she waited at baggage reclaim, just in case her mum was delayed and needed to contact her. To her surprise she had three messages and as she read them her heart twisted with both joy and pain.

Dad sent his love and told her again he was always there for her and she always had a home with him if things didn't work out.

Alex told her how much she was missing her already and Meg sent a simple message sending Dani her love.

Dani snapped her phone shut and hauled her case from the carousel. Walking through passport control, though her heart still ached, it didn't feel as lonely. She felt the phone in her pocket and finally realised they would always be with her.

Once in the car with Francine, Dani's mood lightened. Francine chatted excitedly about her new boutique which was now open and doing well. There was the launch of a new range of clothes to arrange, and now Dani would be part of this one. She also told her how pleased Lou and Nico were that she was back again.

As they crawled through the city traffic, the thrill she had experienced that first time began to bubble up again. It was crowded with people dodging between other people and cars on all sides making whatever progress they could.

Dani peered ahead, still entranced by all she saw. Music from a street band caught her attention, then down a side street there was a scuffle and shouting with banners swinging precariously overhead.

'Another demonstration, I fear,' Francine sighed. 'This city is renowned for its demonstrations. They crowd the streets for any excuse and nobody, I think, knows what for.'

On a wide boulevard Dani could just glimpse the window displays when the car slowed. She had almost forgotten such wonderful shoes and dresses existed. And now she was back with it all and her excitement was growing by the minute.

They turned off down another quieter street and Francine pulled the car up outside a building with a huge oak doorway.

'I have to drop some fabric samples into this office. I'll be only one minute. I think you can wait in the car for me.'

As it was, Francine was gone much longer and Dani was left with little to watch and her mind turned to thoughts of home.

Was it only this morning her dad had hugged her and sent her on her way? His sad smile was imprinted on her mind and her throat tightened.

Had she made the right decision to leave all that was familiar behind and come to a country that was strange and where she knew nobody other than her French family? And she didn't even know them well, either.

Claude had been part of her reason for wanting so much to return — but where was he?

Her mother hadn't mentioned him and Dani had been too afraid to ask because she didn't want to hear the answer she feared she would get. Claude had obviously moved on — as she had told him to.

So now she was here with just her mum and a whole new life which she knew little of and nobody to talk to about it, and suddenly she felt very lonely and very scared.

Nevertheless, when Francine got back into the car and began to chatter to her again, Dani instantly felt better again.

Francine knew the city well and they were soon on the quieter road leading to the district where she had her apartment.

'I think tonight we will not dine out, nor even take the time to cook. I have bought your favourite paté and cheese and some baguette, so we will be able to relax and rest. Will that suit you?'

'It sounds absolutely perfect.' Dani smiled with relief.

★   ★   ★

Once Dani had showered and eaten, tiredness engulfed her. Wearing her pyjamas and snuggled into a corner of the settee, she felt her eyes beginning to droop.

Francine was looking through some paperwork for an early start tomorrow.

'What time will I have to be up?' Dani asked, hoping the answer was not going to be the crack of dawn. She felt drained.

Francine gave her an indulgent smile.

'You may sleep until you wake, my dear. You are exhausted with the journey. I am not a slave driver. You will rest here tomorrow and we will see how you feel then. There's no hurry since you're here for good now. A day or two will make no difference.'

Dani breathed a sigh of relief.

She still hadn't had the courage to ask about Claude and her mother hadn't mentioned him. Now all she wanted was her bed.

★   ★   ★

It seemed as if she was only just up and dressed when Francine was back after a full day's work!

'You look better today. Now I'm the tired one. My feet are killing me in these shoes. I want only to kick them off and sit.'

'Then you do that,' Dani told her. 'I'll make you a nice cup of tea.'

Francine gave a peal of laughter. 'Oh, your wonderful English tea! Yes, oh yes, we will have some. It will make me a new woman, I believe.'

Dani smiled but felt a lump in her throat. Dad wouldn't have reacted like that. It was all different here and what had been fun for holidays seemed strange now she was actually living it. She hoped she would get used to it.

'Tomorrow I have arranged for a day off. We will go shopping and buy you some suitable clothes. I think you'll not want to wear what you brought with you, am I right?'

Dani swallowed hard. Was this really the life she wanted? She thought again of her dad and Meg and Alex. She and Alex had shopped together and been so excited with each purchase and now it wasn't good enough. Fashion to Dani was getting a new pair of jeans in Topshop. Here it was totally different and she wondered if she would ever adjust.

With Claude beside her it would have been fun — but he wasn't going to be beside her. She was sure now that he had gone, and she felt abandoned and alone.

'You look sad,' Francine said, giving Dani a worried look.

'I want to start work, Mum.'

'You're right. Next Monday I will take you to one of my boutiques and you will begin your training.'

Suddenly Dani had to know — and she had to know now!

Standing in the small kitchen, kettle in hand, she faced Francine.

'Mum, what's happened to Claude?'

Francine's expression changed, her face full of compassion as her eyes held Dani's.

'My, dear, I have been afraid of this moment. I hoped you had forgotten him, but in my heart I knew you had not. That is what makes you sad?'

'Has he moved on? Tell me, I need to know.'

Francine placed a steadying hand on her shoulder. 'Yes, he is gone. He left Paris a few weeks after we returned.'

'Why did he go?' Her voice was a whisper.

'I think he was heartbroken to come back without you.'

'But, Mum, I couldn't cope with it at

the time. I couldn't see how I could leave Dad — and Ryan was in a bad way.'

Francine spoke gently.

'He loved you, Dani, and you hurt him badly. I think now he has plunged himself into work to try to forget you.'

Dani nodded. It was what she had feared. Now all that was left was for her to try to do the same.

'Now you have asked I must tell you that I believe he has a lady friend with whom he is seen a lot. You must forget about him, Dani. You have a new life here and soon you will make new friends. You are a beautiful young woman and have your whole life ahead of you.'

All Dani could do was nod.

Francine had been straight with her and she knew she was right. She had made her choice and had nobody to blame but herself.

She couldn't keep changing her mind back and forth like she had, messing up other people's lives. She had to start taking responsibility for her actions. Next Monday she would begin work and she would give it her all.

Again Francine studied her face with concern.

'It hurts now, I know, but it will pass, I promise you. Would you like to stay with Lou and Nico for a while until you feel more like coping?'

Dani straightened and looked at Francine.

'No, Mum. Next week I start work.'

Francine looked pleased. 'You are right. And I have plans for you. Annette who manages one of my Paris boutiques needs an assistant as she is very busy. My clothes are in great demand! I think this will be a good start for you. Annette will train you well and you will get a feel for the clothes and the type of customer we aim for. It will give you time to adjust to your new life here.'

'I'm not going to be a shop assistant, am I?' Dani said in some alarm as she made the tea.

Francine smiled. 'Dear me, no! This

is just a beginning. We have to find out what you are most suited to, let you explore all areas of the business. It cannot be accomplished in one day.'

Dani nodded. 'I'll do my best, Mum. I really want to make a success of this. And working with all those lovely clothes will be a great start.'

'Of course it will and you will be wonderful with our customers. Annette, too, is very sweet and she will love you.'

Francine took her tea through to the living room and Dani stayed in the kitchen to see to their evening meal, her mind a turmoil of troubled thoughts.

Claude was gone from her life.

What if she wasn't up to this work? What if Annette thought her young and gauche? What if the customers were snooty and abrupt? If her mum didn't think her clothes were suitable for this new life, then maybe she wasn't either.

What had she done, giving up her old life, the one she knew, a career she was doing well in and think she could become someone so different?

Leaving the fish she was about to cook on the counter, she grabbed her mobile to phone Alex, then decided against it. Alex was too far away and wouldn't know what to do anyway. No, she had to get on with it and not be such a wimp!

There was one person Dani knew would understand. She found the number she'd stored in her phone weeks ago and felt guilty about not having been in touch before.

Nancy picked up immediately and gasped with surprise when she heard Dani's voice.

'I'm sorry I didn't return your calls,' Dani said.

Nancy quickly jumped in.

'No need. I understand. Where are you?'

They arranged to meet next day in a bar in the centre of the city after her shopping spree with Francine. She could find her own way home. She'd have to start doing that, now that she lived here in Paris.

The bar where they met was noisy with lunchtime office workers, which suited Dani fine as they could sit in a corner and not be overheard.

Francine had taken the parcels of clothes back to the car and told Dani she'd come back for her later. With some difficulty Dani had managed to reassure Francine that she was quite capable of finding her own way back to the apartment.

It was good to see Nancy again and after warm greetings, they settled with glasses of wine and grinned at each other with pleasure. Then Nancy became more serious.

'Claude was devastated when he came back without you, you know,' she said.

'I know. I treated him very badly.'

'He really loved you, Dani. I've never known Claude in such a state.'

Dani felt a lump choking the words in her throat. 'Do you know where he is?' she asked.

'No. He came to see us one evening when we were having a gathering at Maurice's place. He drank too much and Maurice tried to persuade him to stay the night, but he wouldn't. He staggered out into the street. We couldn't stop him.'

'Where did he go?'

'Nobody's heard from him since then. He hasn't been in touch. We're all really worried.'

Dani had difficulty forming the words.

'Mum told me he has a new lady friend.'

Nancy's eyes opened wide. 'No, Dani. He couldn't possibly have. He was crazy about you. I've never known him like that before.'

Dani swallowed a large mouthful of wine. 'Well, he's gone, and there's nothing I can do about it.'

'But Dani, you must do something. Claude loves you — and you still love him, I can tell.'

'But what can I do?'

'Ask your mum where he is?' Nancy said.

Dani shook her head. 'Nancy, there's no point. If he has another girlfriend I'd only be giving myself more heartache.'

Nancy gave her a sympathetic look.

'I'm so sorry, Dani. I felt sure you two were made for each other.'

★   ★   ★

Dressed in an elegant suit and shoes, Francine took Dani to the boutique the following Monday morning. It was situated in one of the fashion districts of Paris. Standing in the big square looking at the large wooden door, Dani thought it a drab building. There were no window displays, just a discreet plaque stating *Francine Sibuet*, her mother's maiden name.

However, as soon as they were inside her eyes opened wide. It was like the reception area of an expensive hotel. Velvet covered sofas were placed around low tables with vases of fresh flowers and expensive glossy magazines. Long gilded mirrors were hung with gossamer drapes. Clothes were draped from velvet hangers with discreet labels stitched into them showing they came from the Francine collection, all displayed with the perfect accessories.

Dani felt a glow of pride that she was to become part of such a prestigious fashion house.

Annette was a little older than Francine, small, blonde and very stylish. She had a warm smile and a bright personality and Dani felt instinctively that she would be a lovely person to work for.

After a few words of introduction Francine left and Annette showed Dani around, chatting all the time, explaining things to Dani, who had difficulty listening as she took in the splendour of it all.

'I think you like what you see,' Annette said with a smile. 'I feel honoured to work in such a place myself. Your mother produces beautiful clothes that are very expensive. Our clientèle expect this luxury. I think you will like to work here, yes?'

'Oh, yes. I just hope I'm up to it.'

'Of course. I can already see a lot of your mother in you.'

★　★　★

It was the beginning of the most exciting few weeks Dani had ever spent. Annette was patient and Dani learned fast. The customers were very rich and some were also quite demanding. Annette handled them politely but firmly and Dani watched and learned.

Between times they unpacked, sorted and displayed new clothes which were delivered in silk garment bags. All the time they chatted amicably.

Dani was in her element. It was hard and tiring work and she went home every night, collapsed in a chair and usually fell asleep.

'I have very good reports from Annette of your progress,' Francine told her over dinner one evening. 'I think you enjoy the work? But you look tired, my dear. You must have a day off.'

'I don't need time off, Mum, I really enjoy every day,' Dani said genuinely.

'That is good.' Francine smiled at her indulgently.

★   ★   ★

It was in the quiet times when she wasn't busy or too tired to think that Dani's mind turned to Claude. He was always in her heart. Where was he? Who was he with? Was he happy? Had she really hurt him so badly? Did he ever think of her?

She tried hard not to have these thoughts and to chase them out by thinking about her career and how lucky she was to have found work she really enjoyed.

Being with Francine again after all these years completed her happiness. When she discussed business with Francine, Claude's name never cropped up. Perhaps her mum didn't know much about his whereabouts or maybe she was just considering her feelings — and Dani was grateful for that. She couldn't have coped with hearing what he was doing. The other name that didn't crop up was Rêve, and Dani could only assume that she had gone too.

What she wasn't prepared for was Annette bringing it up. They were unpacking a new delivery of dresses and chatting about the launch and which models they were to use.

'Thank goodness we do not have that troublesome Rêve this time,' Annette said.

Dani tensed then tried to make herself answer casually. 'I think I met her last time I was here.'

'She was nothing but trouble. Always wanting so much attention!'

'What happened to her?' Dani asked, trying to keep her voice casual.

Annette huffed. 'As soon as Claude went she upped and left also. Left us in quite a dilemma. We had to replace her at such short notice. I think your mother would not consider using her again.'

'Where did she go?' Dani ventured.

'Oh, I expect she followed Claude. She was besotted with him.'

Annette obviously knew nothing of Dani's feelings for Claude. Her mum wouldn't have divulged anything like this to one of her employees.

Dani was struggling but she had to know.

'Did Claude feel the same, do you think?'

Annette gave her a questioning look and Dani feared she had given away too much, but Annette carried on without comment.

'Well, he did seem attracted to her. He let her get away with murder, always took her side. Poor Pierre never stood a chance against the two of them. I think everyone was pleased she went. She was a liability, not worth the trouble.'

'Oh, I think Madame Buffet has

arrived,' Dani said. She was relieved when Annette went to attend to the client and she was left to polish the mirrors and to try to deal with the unbearable hurt she felt inside.

12

The end of another day. Dani dropped her bag in the hall. She was worn out. On her feet all day unpacking clothes, checking invoices, filing accounts then onto the metro and home with all the other tired workers of Paris.

She enjoyed working with Annette and could not have wished for a better manager. Every day she learned more about the business. Tonight all she wanted was to put her feet up and chill.

As usual Francine was still out so she made herself some tea and spread a chunk of bread thickly with honey. It would be ten o'clock at least before they ate a proper meal.

For once she was glad it was the weekend and she could relax. Annette had insisted she must have some time to herself and, much as she loved the job, the thought of a whole Saturday to do nothing did appeal. She kicked off her shoes and settled in her favourite big chair with her food.

Within minutes a key turned in the door and Francine walked briskly into the room, kicking off her shoes and tossing her large bag onto one of the cane chairs.

'We must pack — we leave in half an hour!'

Dani frowned. 'What? Where are we going?'

'It is a surprise for your birthday. Lou and Nico have arranged a party for you tomorrow for all the family. They phoned only an hour ago. I think they do not realise how busy we are here. So we'll drive down tonight then you can relax tomorrow before everyone arrives.'

Dani groaned. 'Mum, do we have to? I was looking forward to a weekend to recover. I don't want a party. My birthday was days ago. We celebrated it then.'

There had been cards and her mum had bought her a Versace tote bag and a silk knit top. They'd opened a bottle of champagne and Francine had taken her to an expensive restaurant for a meal.

Dani hadn't been able to stop thinking how it would have been back in Brandwell with her friends. Dad would have ordered a Chinese and Alex would have come round. Meg always arrived with a card and present. This year she hadn't even seen her dad. And now she had to go through the family thing when all she wanted to do was sleep.

Francine came and sat beside her.

'You are worn out, I can see that. It is hard work you are doing and Annette appreciates how helpful you are. But I think maybe you should have a few days off. One weekend is not enough and I'm sure Annette will agree. She told me you should have more fun and not work so hard. So I think maybe you should stay with Lou and Nico for a short break. It will do no harm. Annette will manage a few days without you.'

'Mum, I don't need a break. I love the work. I just need the weekend.

Please let's stay here.'

'What, and disappoint your grand-parents? I know you don't want that. No, Dani, it is arranged and we must go. You can sleep all the way in the car and all tomorrow morning. I will pack for you so you have nothing to concern yourself with. All that is required is for you to be there.'

There was no fighting it. She had to go.

*   *   *

After several hours' sleep in the car it was good to arrive at the farmhouse and be engulfed in the loving arms of her family. A fire blazed up the chimney and they ate hot soup with crusty bread, the whole house alive with warmth and chatter.

Next morning she was up and out riding on Snowy — trying not to remember the last time, when Claude had raced her on Louis. Though her heart was heavy at the memory she determined nothing was going to spoil these few days with her grandparents.

Yet thoughts of Claude kept intruding. He had told her he loved her. He had pleaded with her. And she knew she would never find love like that ever again.

'You must rest before our guests begin to arrive,' Nico told her as she brought Snowy back into the stable block. 'I will take the horse. You go up to the house and eat. Remember, tonight is your special night.' His smile was indulgent.

She trudged back across the field thinking how everything was the same as last time — yet not the same — the ride, the fussing, the party . . .

The only thing different was that Claude would not be there.

★　★　★

At six o'clock Dani was ready to face the family and friends her grandparents had invited. Francine was elegantly dressed as ever and had given Dani the most exquisite ruby red dress to wear. It was one Dani had raved over when it came into the boutique and Francine had produced it this morning as a complete surprise.

The family arrived in dribs and drabs, each presenting her with an expensive present. Aunt Hermie gave her a gold bracelet and there were some very large cheques and flowers and chocolates. She felt indulged and loved — yet she couldn't help glancing at the door whenever she could without making it obvious, just in case Claude should arrive unexpectedly.

Not that she wanted him to. Not now he had another woman in his life. It would be unbearable. Especially if he brought her with him. She quickly dispelled the thought. Her grandparents wouldn't allow that. By now they must know of her feelings for Claude.

She struggled for a while to keep the smile on her face but was soon carried along with the enjoyment of the evening. Her family were all lovely and everyone wanted her to be happy.

The table was beautifully laid with all the best silver and cut glass and the food, as always, was delicious. Aunt Hermie had made a huge iced cake and had managed to fit on twenty-four candles. Dani blew them all out in one go and everyone cheered.

Dani remained the centre of attention throughout the evening and eventually, after several glasses of wine she felt completely relaxed and enthusiastically told them how she was getting on in the boutique and what she thought about living in Paris and what direction she might take in the fashion business. They were so lovely and warm and kind. How could she possibly want for more?

By the time they had all departed she was glowing with happiness and fell asleep in her big comfy bed with a feeling of complete contentment.

★　★　★

When she woke next morning she lay thinking about the lovely evening she'd had. But now it was over she didn't want to hang around and let intrusive thoughts spoil it. Work was the best thing for her now.

'I really do want to go home with you,' Dani told Francine over breakfast next morning. 'I'm fine now, honestly. Last night was brilliant and I wouldn't have missed it for the world, but now I want to get back to work.'

'No, Dani, it is arranged. You will stay here until next weekend when I will return for you. Lou and Nico will be so disappointed if you do not stay.'

Dani shook her head in despair. It was true. Her grandparents adored her and they hadn't seen much of her since she'd come to France. If her mum decided she needed a break then perhaps she could enjoy relaxing here for a week.

★   ★   ★

'Lou, you don't need to take me out every day. I'm happy just being here. I can ride Snowy and do some reading to improve my French.'

Lou stood determined. 'Your French is already very good, Dani, and we enjoy taking you out. Charente is a beautiful region and there is a lot to see. I think you are spending too much time between that boutique and the apartment.'

It was no good arguing and she enjoyed being out and about with them again, exploring all the favourite haunts they had taken her to when she had come for holidays as a child.

'Today we go to Verteuil. You like the river there, and the beautiful chateau and we can eat out in this lovely autumn sunshine at the café overlooking the river. You would enjoy that I think, a nice relaxing day.'

'Yes, I remember. It's a long drive, though.'

'Everywhere in this very large country is far, not as it is in your small

271

island. But we have the car. It will not take too long.'

Dani didn't mind the drive as there was always so much to see and it kept her mind occupied. She loved the pretty villages they passed through and the fields of sunflowers and the gentle rolling countryside.

So the week progressed. Each day another outing. Nanteuil with its narrow streets, houses of warm stone rising steeply on either side, brown shutters and window boxes of colourful flowers. They found a bric-a-brac sale and Lou bought some jugs.

'Here we see the Lavoir where the people used to do their washing in the river many years ago,' Lou explained as they explored the town.

'I'm glad we don't have to do it like that now,' Dani laughed.

When they got back to the car Nico noticed a praying mantis perched on the wheel and he put it carefully on the back of his hand so that Dani could examine it. Her first thought was how her dad would have loved to see this strangely beautiful insect.

In Champagne Mouton, Lou took Dani to a dress shop and bought her some tops that Alex would have died for. She wished she could have shown them to her.

Then they bought mussels from the market and Lou promised to show her how to make them into moule, a delicious soup with onions, potatoes, wine and cream. Her mouth watered at the thought of dipping the fresh crusty bread into it when they sat around the farmhouse table for dinner that night.

As they strolled through the village Dani stopped to look at a lovely cottage rendered a pale lemon. 'I love the way so many houses are pastel with those big heavy doors.' she said. 'I'd forgotten how all the villages seem to have a chateau and a river running through them.'

'Is it so different in England?' Lou asked her.

'Everything is different in England,'

Dani said and felt a catch in her voice.

Lou noticed. 'You are missing home, I think.'

Dani was quick to reassure her. 'No, Lou, I love France and it's where I want to be. This is my home now.' But Lou didn't look convinced and Dani sighed. 'I do miss Dad and my friends.'

And Claude, she thought.

Lou patted her hand. 'It will take time for you to settle. Be patient, my dear.'

As they walked along the river in the late October sunshine Nico took her arm.

'Your mother will return the day after tomorrow. Then you must go back to Paris. You are impatient to be away, I think,'

'Oh, no, I've really enjoyed staying with you.'

'I know, my dear, but you are keen to get back to work. I understand. I was the same at your age. This, too, happened for me. It was a very smart tailors for gentlemen. I was sixteen when I started and the pay was very poor. But I knew immediately it was the world in which I would spend my life.'

Dani looked at him. His eyes were bright with the memory.

'It's what I want, too,' she told him.

'Well, your mother has several boutiques now. I think soon you will be managing one of them. She tells me you are doing very well. Annette is pleased with you. But are you happy here?' His face became more serious.

She smiled up at him. 'Yes, I'm happy, although I miss my friends sometimes.'

'But I think you also miss someone else, someone who is in France.'

She could feel the tears coming and blinked to keep them at bay.

'Have you not tried to contact him to ask him how he feels?'

'No. Mum said I should forget about him, that he's moved on.'

'Your mother is trying to spare your feelings. Is it not worth the risk? You may get hurt, but if you do not try you will never know.'

She nodded. 'I don't think I can.'

'Think about it. You will find the strength.'

He hugged her close then pointed to some ducks on the river and changed the subject.

'The sunflowers look so sad now,' Lou said, pointing to the drooping heads as they drove home. 'In summer they hold their heads high and look happy.'

Dani stared out of the window. Their drooping heads did look sad. Maybe one day she would be able to forget Claude and hold her head high.

* * *

That evening after they'd finished the fish moule, Lou tried to get Dani to eat some cheese. 'You are so thin, Dani. You must eat more. Are you sure you are happy here?'

'Yes, I enjoy the work and I love being with Mum. I'll get used to it.'

'But why are you sad, my dear? You must not do this to please your mother. She would not wish that. If you feel you have made a mistake then you must say so. All is not lost. You can go back to England if that is what will make you happy.'

Go back — did she really want to go back? What was there to go back for now anyway? Claude wasn't waiting for her in Brandwell. He wasn't waiting for her anywhere!

Dani didn't think she could approach him as Nico had suggested. Her mum had told her it was over and that was that. She couldn't bear any more disappointment and heartache. No, she might as well carry on here and try to be successful in a business she loved.

'We have one last treat for you before you go home, then,' Lou told her. 'Tomorrow we go to Confolens for a special meal in a lovely restaurant by the river, then next day your mother will come and we must hand you back — for now, at least.'

★   ★   ★

It was a beautiful spot facing the castle on the river and a table had been reserved for them outside in the sunshine, which was still warm even in mid October. Lou had disappeared to talk to a friend she had spotted, and Nico was talking to the owner of the restaurant.

Dani sipped her glass of wine and leaned back to enjoy the warmth of the sun on her face. On Monday she would be hard at work again and she was looking forward to it. But today she was determined to relax and enjoy the moment. Closing her eyes against the glare she let her mind drift. It had been a good week and she did feel better for it.

When she opened her eyes she saw Nico carrying a tray of drinks towards the table. Then she blinked and stared, and then looked again.

Close behind him was a face from her dreams, smiling that smile she thought she would never see again!

She looked at Lou, who was now standing beside her. She was smiling, and Nico was grinning at her.

Then those eyes she had so much wanted to see were looking straight into hers. They weren't smiling — but they were full of love and passion.

It was Claude. Claude was here!

He took her hands in his and kissed each cheek. 'Dani, it is so good to see you again.'

Nico pulled out a seat while Dani continued to look from one to the other in confusion.

Lou and Nico had arranged this! This was what it was all about, this meal. Why had Claude gone along with it? Claude had another woman in his life now. Francine had told her to forget about him. Nico had wanted her to talk to Claude — but not like this, in such a public place and not being prepared for it!

She tried to get up but her legs were useless, anchored to the ground under the table. She looked away from their smiling faces and down at the table. What she wanted at this moment more than anything was to be home safe with her dad and her friends.

'Dani, are you all right?' Claude asked in his soft voice.

Nico and Lou had begun to look worried.

Dani managed to get to her feet and backed away from the table on shaking legs. The chair behind her fell backwards with a clatter. Claude was on his feet and took her arm. She shrugged it away and began to walk away quickly, down to the river, struggling with the hurt inside her.

Claude followed and took hold of her elbow to stop her. 'Why are you running away?'

She turned and looked at him through her tears.

'I'm sorry. I felt dizzy . . . must be the wine . . . ' she managed to croak.

He shook his head and held her gaze, knowing something was wrong. 'Let us go back to the table and sit down.'

She didn't know what else to do. She was trying so hard to keep her emotions in check.

Lou pulled out a chair next to her and Nico put a glass of water in front of her then started to ask Claude about the business.

Claude turned to Dani, smiling.

'He will not let go, your grandfather. I tell him not to worry; that's what he pays me to do now. But he wants to know what I'm doing. I think he does not trust me.'

'That is quite untrue. I have known you too long for that. I like to keep my brain working. You will not object to humouring an old man, I think.'

'You will never be old, Nico. You will outlive us all.'

They were trying to bring some normality to the situation, obviously shocked at her reaction.

Their voices blurred into a wall of sound which shielded her from the intensity of Claude's presence and allowed her to recover some degree of equilibrium. Nico must have realised now that the surprise hadn't been such a good idea, and kept glancing at her with concern.

Seeing Claude again had ignited all Dani's old feelings for him. Yet she knew the way she had reacted on seeing him was totally childish and she felt ashamed. She had to regain control quickly and act in a more mature way. So she put a smile on her face and tried to enter into the conversation.

The food arrived, fresh grilled fish with a light salad and crusty bread. The meal seemed to go on for ever and slowly Dani began to accept the situation and feel more comfortable in Claude's presence. He was a lovely man and the attraction was as strong as ever. Feelings were returning that she thought she had managed to overcome and seeing him again caused her to remember how close they had been.

Now they'd been forced together again she began to wish they could have some time alone to talk. There were things she wanted to explain, to try to clear up any misunderstandings. Then, perhaps, they could remain friends. If he was still working in the family business that was important.

Eventually Nico paid the bill and made to leave. Claude stood up and looked uncertainly at Dani.

'I have the whole afternoon free which is a rare treat for me. I would like to spend it with you, Dani. If you would like that, too?'

Dani felt her whole body fill with relief and joy. She would have her chance to talk to him alone.

'What would you like to do, Dani?' Lou asked.

Claude gave her a pleading look. 'I can take you home later if you will spend this afternoon with me. I should very much like that. But if you wish to return with your grandparents . . . '

'No, it would be good to spend some time with you.' She struggled to make it sound casual and hoped she hadn't conveyed her true feelings. She didn't want him to get the wrong idea.

He had another woman in his life now and she mustn't forget that. Yet the last thing she wanted was to say goodbye to him again without the chance of putting things right between them.

She had to at least try to explain. She owed him that much. He'd been incredibly patient and didn't deserve the way she had treated him.

Claude turned to Lou. 'I will take good care of her and return her to you this evening.'

Claude shook hands with Nico and kissed Lou on both cheeks.

Warmth spread through Dani when Claude took her hand to steady her as he led her down the river bank onto the path. It felt so right, and her heart twisted painfully for what she had thrown away. Claude meant everything to her. How was she ever going to live without him? But if she wanted them to be friends she had to pull herself together or this afternoon would be embarrassing for both of them.

'How did you know I would be here?' she asked him, withdrawing her hand from his as they reached level ground and trying with all her strength to make her voice sound casual.

He looked at her with a sheepish grin.

'Lou told me. She sometimes comes to the factory where we make the clothes.'

'But my mum said you'd moved far away.'

'Dani, this is far away. It's where I started work for your grandfather making clothes for his rich clients. Now his business is very large and successful and he is training me to take over here so he can retire. I'm sure you know all that.'

Dani shrugged, embarrassed.

'I don't know much about it at all. I hear them talking but have never taken a lot of interest in how it started. So how did you come to be working with Mum?'

'When your mother came back to France and began to expand the business in Paris, Nico sent me there to support her. That was how I came to be there when you first met me. But my home is here. As you know, my parents live just a few miles away, so now I'm back and working here once more.'

'But Nico won't retire, will he?'

'No, he keeps an eye on things. I admire him. He has taught me everything I know and I always listen to his advice.'

She was beginning to feel relaxed and, as they chatted, it seemed they had never been apart.

'Mum must really miss you now,' Dani said.

'She understood the situation,' was all he said.

Dani didn't know what to say after this. There was an awkward silence as they ducked under a bridge over the river. Once they'd negotiated this difficult bit of the path she stopped him.

'Claude, I'm really sorry I didn't write back. I . . . '

Her voice faltered.

'You have nothing to explain and you

have nothing to be sorry about. You were under a lot of stress and I understood. But when Lou told me you were here, I had to see you. So here I am.'

Her heart was twisting inside her. It just felt so good to be with him again. There were no words to explain. It was all too painful.

As they began to walk again, it seemed they were both trying to keep things under control. There was so much to talk about, things she wanted to share with him, the problems she'd had to face, but she didn't know where to start. On the surface he was offering friendship and nothing more. Yet beneath that she felt something stronger, yet couldn't find a way of reaching it.

He began to ask about her job with Annette.

'I really like working there. I'm learning a lot about the fashion world,' she said, relieved the tension had passed and the conversation become more general again.

'It was a very good place for you to

start,' he agreed. 'And have you decided in what direction you may want to move eventually?'

'I think I'd like to manage a boutique one day,' she said.

'Your mother seems intent on opening many so you have every opportunity.'

'I have a lot to learn before that happens.'

'I'm sure you'll learn quickly and Annette is very knowledgeable. You could not be in better hands.'

'I enjoy meeting the customers. They're an interesting lot. Some really make me laugh. Annette and I often talk about them and she tells me who they are.'

As the afternoon went along Dani began to enjoy their conversation and, as the talk became natural again, she remembered how much she had always enjoyed his company.

They had coffee sitting out in the sunshine and then made their way back into the town where Claude had left his car.

However, the tension began to grow

again as it became clear he was about to take her back home. Walking through the streets towards the car park he kept looking at Dani as if there were things he wanted to say but didn't know whether it was appropriate. They kept starting sentences and stopping, each feeling awkward.

In the end Dani gave up.

He had someone else in his life and she had no business upsetting that relationship. If that was the subject he was trying to broach, she didn't want to hear about it. Best to keep the conversation neutral. She wanted the afternoon to draw to a close quickly now. The tension was becoming unbearable.

He had obviously come to the same conclusion.

On the drive back to the farmhouse, they both fell into silence.

When he stopped to let her out they looked at each other and there was sorrow in that look. Nothing had been resolved. They hadn't talked about anything that mattered. Dani knew they wouldn't have a chance like this again, and in her heart she knew there was no point anyway. They'd both moved on. They had separate lives. There was nothing to discuss.

He went in with her and spoke with Nico about work. After what seemed an age he got up and said his goodbyes to Lou.

Dani went out to the car with him and as they stood uncertainly beside it his eyes held hers just a fraction too long. She looked away then said a quick goodbye and walked back up to the house. She knew she would not be able to sustain a lengthy farewell.

This was the last time they would spend time together like this. Best get it over quickly. She could feel he was standing watching her go and she had never felt so wretched. The door was open and she forced herself to go inside without looking back.

Then she burst into tears.

Lou was at her side. She took her into the kitchen and sat beside her holding her hand until her sobbing subsided.

'I think perhaps we made a mistake today,' Lou said gently.

Dani nodded and they hugged each other, both feeling deep sadness.

13

It was two weeks after she had returned to Paris when Francine told her Claude was to come back to help launch their new range of clothes.

'He is so good at organising these things,' she told Dani. 'Nico is to take over in Convolens for the time being. It will be good for him to get involved again. I'm not sure he is ready for retirement yet.'

Dani felt her body stiffen and knew she must have looked alarmed because Francine's face took on a concerned look.

'We have to face this problem, my dear. Claude is part of this business. I know it is hurtful for you but I cannot prevent it. I think in time you will learn to cope.'

Dani quickly pulled herself together. 'I know, Mum. Of course I can cope.'

She'd been trying ever since she got back from her stay with Lou and Nico to put him out of her mind, putting in all the hours she could with Annette in the boutique.

Now he was coming back.

She kept telling herself they probably wouldn't see each other as it was unlikely their paths would cross. But knowing he was in Paris and working with Francine was unsettling.

Next day Dani went in to work determined to put Claude completely out of her mind.

She felt safe in the boutique, for he would have no cause to come in there. After stowing away some catalogues she began to make their mid-morning coffee in a relaxed mood.

A huge box arrived. Annette was tidying magazines and arranging flowers on one of the low tables so Dani took the box into one of the changing rooms and began to unpack a beautiful evening gown for one of their customers who was due for a fitting later that morning.

Annette came through and watched as Dani hung it on the velvet hanger and smoothed out the draped skirt. They both sighed and admired the simplicity of the dress, the elegant lines and the rich ruby colour.

'It will suit Madame Buffet to perfection,' Annette said.

They both looked through the curtained cubicle when the door opened.

Dani felt the blood drain from her face and gripped the chair in front of her.

Claude stood uncertainly just inside, handsome as ever in beige chinos and a crisp white shirt. His dark eyes devoured her and an irrational joy fizzed through her body at the sight of him. Then her heart began thumping and try as she would she could not control it.

Annette went to greet him.

'I hope you don't mind me walking in unannounced,' he said. 'The door was ajar so I took the liberty as I could see you two ladies were busy.'

'You are always welcome,' Annette

told him. 'I heard you were back. Francine will be happier now that she knows you are on the job again.'

This seemed to relax him and they began to chat, giving Dani time to recover.

She tried to steady her shaking hands as she hung the dress on a hook in the fitting room ready for Madame Buffet to try on. She hoped she would arrive soon so that she could busy herself helping the customer into the dress.

She had to get to grips with the situation. She couldn't afford to give into these feelings.

After arranging accessories to go with the dress and making sure the mirror was at the right angle, she knew she had to come out. There were other orders to be attended to and she couldn't hide away all day.

Annette was showing Claude a range of satin shoes in a catalogue. Then she brought out a box with samples in. 'I think they may complement our new line in evening wear.'

He examined them and seemed to

approve. Then his eyes were on Dani again and, as he held her gaze, that something special passed between them. It was difficult to look away but he had already turned to Annette.

'I wondered if you could spare this young lady for the afternoon. I would like to take her out for lunch.' There was a twinkle in his eye as he glanced back at Dani.

'No, Annette needs me,' Dani said more sharply than was necessary. 'We have an important customer coming for a fitting. She's due any minute.'

How could she spend an afternoon with him feeling as she did?

Annette shook her head and grinned. 'This girl, she thinks I cannot do without her.' She turned to Dani. 'My dear, I can manage Madame Buffet. She is one of our oldest customers and I have known her a very long time.'

'But I need to learn how these fittings are done,' Dani said, anxious to avoid Claude.

'You will learn in time. It is not

necessary for you to watch every one,' Annette said lightly. She turned to Claude. 'You take this young lady for lunch. It will give me some time with my friend, Madame Buffet. We will have coffee and talk a while. This girl works so hard, never sits down, never eats. She deserves an afternoon off.'

'Thank you, Annette. That is good to hear as I do not intend to bring her back this afternoon.'

He winked at Annette and she blushed and shooed him away.

Annette began to clear away the packaging the dress had arrived in. 'Off you go and have a lovely afternoon. You do not get an invitation like this every day. A handsome man wanting to take you for lunch. I do not expect you back until tomorrow morning.'

There seemed no alternative but for Dani to get her jacket and join Claude. She thanked Annette and walked out through the door he was holding open for her, making sure she did not brush against him.

Once outside in the square he stopped and turned towards her. 'I think you do not want to come to lunch with me.' He was regarding her steadily, concern etched on his face.

She swallowed hard and hoped her voice would not let her down.

'Of course. It's very kind of you to ask. I was just worried about leaving Annette on her own.'

His dark eyes studied her keenly.

As they walked along, Dani was struggling with the turmoil his closeness was stirring in her. When their arms momentarily touched, a shiver ran down her spine and she quickly moved to put a distance between them. It would have been so natural to slip her hand into his. But she knew she could not afford to have these feelings. If he was making this effort at friendship then she had to do the same.

They walked on in awkward silence for some time until Dani felt she had to break it.

'How come you're free today? I thought

it was all panic about this launch,' she said, trying to sound casual.

'That's true, but your mother told me to take you off for the afternoon and who am I to argue?' His lips twitched into a hint of a smile.

So that was the reason he was here. Her mother had got them together to make sure there would be no awkwardness to interfere with the business. She had told Dani she had to learn to cope with the situation and this was her way of achieving this. Dani wished Francine would keep out of it and let them sort it out between themselves. Then she realised that was exactly what this afternoon would allow them to do — and she had to try to make it work.

They lunched in a small bistro just off the square and after a couple of glasses of wine relaxed into an easy familiarity. They talked about the business, about the launch of the new line in clothes. He amused her with tales of Nico and how getting back to running the business had given him a new lease of life. She told him how much she was enjoying her work with Annette and how much more fun it was than working in the bank. It was good to be with him again. He was warm and kind and good company and Dani almost managed to believe that eventually they could be friends.

The lunch extended until late in the afternoon and as the blue sky began to mellow to a deeper shade they were still sitting outside chatting and sipping wine.

'I don't like these dark days of late October,' she said wistfully.

Claude gave her a warm smile. 'But they do have their advantage. You have seen the Seine in sunshine, and now you will see it in its magical evening mood.' He stood up and called the waiter over for the bill, then looked down at her as she pulled on her jacket, his eyes searching hers. 'We could take a boat trip down the river.' He hesitated. 'That is if you would like.'

His anxious look warmed her heart.

He was always so gallant. But she wasn't sure.

'Shouldn't we be getting back? Mum will be wondering where I've got to.'

His face clouded.

'I will take you home if that is what you wish, but I'm sure your mother won't worry just yet.'

Warning bells were ringing, yet the thought of cruising down the Seine with Claude was too much to resist. It had turned out to be a lovely day. Despite everything they had managed to enjoy each other's company. Claude had promised to take her on a boat trip on the Seine when she'd first arrived in Paris. So long as she was careful to keep her emotions in check she thought she could still enjoy it. Then he could take her home and she would know she could cope with whatever situation presented itself.

'OK, we'll go on the Seine,' she agreed.

They found a tourist boat just about to leave. Claude helped her on board and as their fingers touched a tiny electric shock passed between them. His look told her he had felt it too.

Squashed up very close on a long seat, his nearness both disturbed and excited her. She longed for him to slip his arm round her and draw her closer yet knew this could not happen. So she allowed herself a few moments of indulgent pleasure, knowing it was harmless as nothing could come of it.

As they cruised down the river and under the bridges silver moonlight rippled the water and illuminated buildings glowed golden against the darkening sky.

Dani sighed. 'Paris is amazing.'

When the lady sitting next to her got up Dani edged away a little from Claude's side and he straightened in his seat. It was so hard not to relax into the romance of the night. Feelings were surging through her. Here she was, sitting beside the man she had once hoped to spend the rest of her life with, cruising down the Seine in the moonlight — and knowing his heart lay elsewhere.

When he helped her off the boat they stood very close for a moment, mesmerised by the beauty of the moonlight on the water and the glorious buildings in all their illuminated splendour.

As they progressed along the path away from the quay Claude wound his arm round her waist, pulled her to him and kissed her cheek. It caught her off-guard and her fingers went the spot where his lips had touched her.

'Claude we shouldn't be doing this,' she said gently, pulling away.

He let her go but turned to stand in front of her, passion distorting his face.

'I'm sorry, Dani. I did not mean to upset you. I thought you were feeling as I am.'

She was struggling for composure.

'What does it matter what I feel? We can't do this. It isn't right.'

He frowned. 'Why is it not right?'

She took a deep breath. 'Because you have someone else now.'

There was a sharp shift in his expression and his grip on her arm was

303

almost painful, his dark eyes blazing.

'What are you saying? Who says I have someone else?'

She stared at him, her whole body shaking now. 'My mum told me.'

An angry passion distorted his face. 'Then she is mistaken. I do not have anyone else.'

Confused relief flooded her as their eyes held each other, his dark and intense in the moonlight.

'But Mum said you had a new lady friend, a model — that you were going out together.'

She could hardly form the words, her mouth was trembling so much. It was excitement and disbelief and hope all churning inside her. The intensity of his gaze almost took her breath away yet she carried on burbling and couldn't stop.

'I don't blame you. I told you to go home and to forget about me.'

His anger was gone as he pulled her to him and put a finger to her lips to silence her.

'Dani, these are rumours. Your mother has heard rumours only.'

Love and longing were surging through her yet she had to be sure.

'But rumours don't start from nothing . . . '

He held both her hands in his and she stared down mutely at them. They were warm and firm. Then he lifted her chin so that she was forced to look at him.

'Dani, listen to me. It happens all the time in this business. The fashion business is pressurised. All the time I work with these girls, and maybe I pay one of the models too much attention. Everyone is wanting gossip. I look at a pretty girl, get her a drink and next thing I am to marry her!'

She pulled away. 'So there is someone else?'

Anger flashed in his eyes and she hardly dared breathe while she waited for him to speak.

'Dani, I told you when you first went back home that I would wait for you. I am waiting still . . . '

A wild joy shot through her.

'You mean it? You don't have anyone special?'

'Yes, I *do* have someone special,' he said drawing her closer once again.

'But — '

He silenced her with a whisper of a kiss.

'It is *you*, Dani. You have been special to me since I first set eyes on you. Nothing has changed this for me.' Then he drew away from her. 'But what about you, Dani? You had someone special, I think. That is the reason you did not want to return to Paris — and me.'

His voice was thick with passion and her heart sank at the memory.

'Claude, I'm so sorry. I was upset. My dad wasn't well and he was involved in some trouble at his school.'

'And you were concerned for your friend, Ryan. You did not want to leave him.'

She took a deep breath. 'Ryan and I

went to the same school. I had a crush on him. We went out together for a long time, and he was there for me when I needed him. But we grew apart. When he had that accident I thought it was because of me, because I no longer wanted to be with him.'

Claude stood uncertainly in front of her, his eyes searching hers, his expression grave.

'And now? Dani,' he said gently but firmly. 'I really need to know.'

She held his gaze and spoke in the steadiest voice she could manage. 'Claude, it was over with Ryan before I even met you.'

He relaxed slightly but concern still etched his features.

'And what about us, Dani? Do you think now that we can be more than friends?' His clipped voice told her how emotional he was.

'Oh, yes! We always have been.'

As she moved towards him he enfolded her in his arms and a feeling of pure joy spread through her. She clung to him, never wanting to leave the security they held.

When she drew away a little to look at him his eyes were full of love. Slowly a smile spread over his face and he pulled her to him and kissed her with a deep passion.

Eventually they made their way back into the city, arms round each other, stopping every now and again to kiss, hardly able to believe how everything had changed, hardly taking their eyes off each other.

Once back in the noise and bustle Claude took his arm from round her waist and grabbed her hand, his eyes taking on a mischievous glint.

'It is still early and we do not have to return home yet. I have an idea.'

Next thing they were on top of a tourist bus.

'Now I show you why Paris is called the City of Lights,' Claude said.

This time they sat as close as they could as the bus slowly meandered through brightly lit streets and squares.

Dani felt more alive than she had in years. When the Eiffel Tower appeared in all its brilliant white-illuminated glory she was on the edge of her seat, excitement and joy bubbling up inside her.

'It was the tallest building in the world for many years,' Claude explained. 'Now we see the tomb of the most famous Frenchman in history. Do you know who that is?'

'Napoleon, of course,' she teased, squeezing his hand. He pulled her even closer and hugged her tight as they toured down tree lined boulevards alive with cafés and bars and shops.

Claude pointed down a long tree-lined avenue with lights sparkling in the foliage.

'That is the most famous avenue in the world, The Champs Elysées.' There was pride in his voice. 'And look to the end and you will see The Arc de Triomphe.'

The towering stone arch glowing golden against the dark sky brought tears to her eyes and she had to pinch herself to believe it was real. She'd walked down there many times, but by night it was different — especially with the man she loved by her side.

She turned to Claude and in a trembling voice murmured, 'Oh Claude, I'm so happy.'

He seemed to be struggling for composure himself and squeezed her a little tighter.

The bus came to a stop and Claude took her hand as they got off.

'And now one more treat — then I'm afraid I must take you home.'

They were standing outside the Moulin Rouge and he was drawing her inside.

'Now we see that famous show you have heard of. The Moulin Rouge is the Parisian temple of the can-can. You were impressed to see the outside of the theatre, as I remember. Inside is much more fun.'

He was grinning at her surprise.

The show was a spectacle of light and colour, music and dance.

When they came out into the night again Paris was still bursting with life.

Back on the metro she leaned on Claude's arm, completely satiated with sheer pleasure. She would never forget this night as long as she lived.

Her future now held a promise of all she could possibly have wished for.

★　★　★

Claude left her at the door of the apartment.

'I must go home, now, Dani. I do not want anything to follow to spoil such a special evening and I'm sure your mother will want to hear everything from you alone.'

She understood exactly how he felt; she felt the same. 'Will I see you tomorrow?' she asked.

'Yes, my sweetheart — and every day, for ever,' he whispered. He kissed her gently, then reluctantly let her go.

As soon as she walked into the apartment Francine came to her with a warm smile and a sparkle in her eyes.

'You have enjoyed today?' she asked.

Dani threw herself into waiting arms.

'Mum, I've had the most wonderful day of my life!'

Francine hugged her tightly. 'I am very happy for you, my darling.'

'Mum, what made you change your mind? I mean, getting me and Claude together today. I thought you didn't want me to see him again. You said he had someone else.'

'Yes, that was what I'd been led to believe. But I was mistaken and I wanted to put it right. You are cross with me?'

Dani hugged her mum even tighter.

'Tonight, I couldn't be cross if I tried,' she said.

We do hope that you have enjoyed reading this large print book.

Did you know that all of our titles are available for purchase?

We publish a wide range of high quality large print books including:
Romances, Mysteries, Classics
General Fiction
Non Fiction and Westerns

Special interest titles available in large print are:
The Little Oxford Dictionary
Music Book, Song Book
Hymn Book, Service Book

Also available from us courtesy of Oxford University Press:
Young Readers' Dictionary
(large print edition)
Young Readers' Thesaurus
(large print edition)

For further information or a free brochure, please contact us at:
Ulverscroft Large Print Books Ltd.,
The Green, Bradgate Road, Anstey,
Leicester, LE7 7FU, England.
Tel: (00 44) **0116 236 4325**
Fax: (00 44) **0116 234 0205**

A LITTLE BIT OF CHRISTMAS MAGIC

Kirsty Ferry

As a wedding planner at Carrick Park Hotel, Ailsa McCormack is organising a Christmas Day wedding at the expense of her own holiday. Not that she minds. She's always been fascinated by the place and its past occupants; particularly the beautiful and tragic Ella Carrick, whose striking portrait still hangs at the top of the stairs. And then an encounter with a tall, handsome and strangely familiar man in the drawing room on Christmas Eve sets off a chain of events that transforms Ailsa's lonely Christmas into a magical occasion . . .